TRACY BILEN

Whisper

mirette

To Beverly and Ron
True love is eternal

One

OLIVIA

꧁꧂

My dad used to tell me there are people inside of marbles. They were always talking to him. Whenever I wanted to play a game, he would pick the one with marbles. Only we wouldn't actually move the marbles. My dad would just stare at them. Finally I stopped asking to play games. But that didn't matter. My dad would still get out the game with the marbles, and he'd put the marbles in their little resting spots and watch them. And listen.

At Samantha's house, her three-year-old sister, Cara, is playing a marble game with one of her friends. They're off in a corner by themselves, probably wondering why all these people are stuffed inside the house, wearing dark clothes, crying randomly, and talking in hushed voices. Cara wasn't at Samantha's funeral. Does she understand that her sister is never coming home?

I move away from Cara and fill a plate with cubes of cheese, triangles

1

of salami, and round crackers. I chew, swallow, and make small talk. But mostly I just stare out the window at the pool and remember the last time I was here. Sixth grade. A pool party for Samantha's birthday. She and I were friends then. We stopped being friends sometime in seventh grade. I think it had something to do with green slime, a ham sandwich, and a guy we both liked, though I'm not really sure anymore. It all seems pretty stupid now, which gives me a lumpy ache in my throat, and makes me feel like a fraud for being here. But the whole junior class was at the funeral, all ninety-eight of us.

Make that ninety-seven.

Plus a good part of the rest of the high school. And although not everyone made their way here after the funeral, the house is still packed, with people spilled out onto the lawn, hovering by the pool, and clutching their paper plates as if they're life preservers.

My best friend, Julia, slides up next to me. Her chestnut brown hair is arranged in its usual French braid, except a lot of strands that she missed are poking out today. She takes a loose bit and wraps it around her finger.

"Brings back memories, huh?" she says, following my gaze to the pool. "Remember that sleepover in sixth grade?"

"Yeah, that was fun." Except now my brain jumps right from *sleepover* to *sweet dreams. The Sweet Dreams Strangler.*

I shake my head, trying to blot out the images seared into my mind by the news media. Images of Samantha, lying in a field wearing a beautiful dress, her head on a pillow, hair neatly arranged, hands folded.

Beautiful. But dead. Strangled. I don't know what to say, even to Julia. I look back out the window. A cardinal is perched on the feeder, picking through seeds, scattering debris on the ground.

"It sure is stuffy in here," Julia says.

I'm about to agree when a wall of cold air hits me. "Mrs. Young

2

must have read your mind. Wow. That feels good."

Julia scrunches up her face. "What are you talking about?"

"The air. She turned on the air. Don't you feel it?"

"No. Are you under a vent or something?" Julia peers up at the ceiling.

"Here, switch places with me."

"It's just as hot here—"

"It's just as cold—"

We say it at the same time. "I guess it's just your wishful thinking." Julia pats my shoulder. "Enjoy. I'm going to get some more to drink."

I nod and head across the room, by the TV, where hopefully it's warmer.

Goose bumps pop up on my arms. I rub them, but it doesn't help.

Next to me Josh Wallace tosses a cube of cheese into his mouth. Is that sweat dripping off his forehead? Why am I the only one shivering?

I spot a decorative blanket on the couch. Should I? I tap Marcus on the shoulder. "Sorry, could you lean forward? I just need to get something behind you." I tug at the blanket and drape it over my shoulders.

Julia is back with a drink in her hand. "Why do you have a blanket wrapped around you? Are you feeling okay?"

"Not really," I answer. "What's that noise?"

"What noise?"

"That buzzing sound. Is that the TV? Maybe someone turned it on without switching on the cable box." I fumble with the buttons on the TV. An image flashes across the screen, and a voice blares.

Funeral services were held today for Samantha Young, the fourth victim of the Sweet Dreams Strangler.

Mrs. Young hovers in the doorway between the kitchen and the living room. All the color drains from her face.

I can't seem to move. Julia turns off the TV. The buzzing grows louder, and then I realize that it's voices I'm hearing, lots of them, all blending together into one big buzzing sound.

And then the buzzing fades away until I hear only one voice.

Olivia.

It's not real. I know it's not real.

Olivia.

It's not real because the voice is Samantha's, and Samantha is dead.

Olivia!

It's not real because the voice is not coming from a person. It's coming from a fricking figurine on the mantel. From a yellow bird with black wings and a black head. I pick up the figurine, and I hold it in my hands. *This is what my dad meant when he said there were people living in marbles.* And then it speaks again.

Olivia! Stop him!

Even though I'm kind of expecting it, Samantha's voice scares me all the same. It makes me jump and my hands open up and that figurine smashes on the floor and breaks. And I'm a little glad because maybe now the voice will stop. But suddenly I'm burning up, the salami and cheese rumbles around in my stomach, and before I can sit, the room spins all around me and darkness sets in.

Two

JACOB

"Why did you bring all these broken drumsticks?" my mom asks, pulling a coffee can full of them out of the moving box. She picks one up and squints, reading the writing on the side. "Hysteria?"

If she hadn't ditched my dad and me four years ago, she'd know that I always write the name of the song I was playing and the date when a stick breaks. I'm just about to explain it to her when she says, "It took a week, but you're finally all unpacked. Not bad. Well, I'll leave you to it. I've got to get back to the case."

Big fucking surprise. It's always about the case. Once upon a time my brother was the case. Now it's someone else's kid. Or spouse. Or whatever. Anything so my mom doesn't have to face the people still in her own life. My dad gave up trying to matter to her a long time ago. That's when he and I moved to northern Michigan. My dad's a day trader. He buys and sells stocks on his laptop. You can pretty much do that from anywhere. Except from where you're not wanted. We were doing fine. Then my dad got himself a new wife. And I got into a car with my drunken best friend.

Okay, yeah, I was drunk too. We hit a tree in Ricky's piece-of-shit car that's too old to have airbags. And yeah, I wasn't wearing a seatbelt. So I cracked my head against the dashboard. And I guess I passed out. From the conk in the head or the booze, I'm not sure which. I'm pretty much okay now except for the occasional pounding headache and some freaky-ass dreams. And the fact that my parents actually spoke to each other and decided I should move in with my mom. Get a change of scenery. Get away from my jackass friends.

I shuffle after my mom. I don't know why we bothered unpacking that last box. My mom will realize soon enough that she doesn't want to deal with me and my crap, and I'll be on a plane out of here.

In the kitchen, I pour myself a glass of ginger ale, missing the beer that my dad used to have piled in the fridge, free for the taking. Then I score some chips and M&M's from the counter. In clearing off a space on the table for my snack, I knock a file folder on the floor, and papers spill out everywhere.

"Seriously, Jacob?" my mom says, pissed. Hey, maybe if I dump my drink all over the papers, I can get myself shipped back home in time for dinner. Well, at least I could be in Pittsburgh in time to get on a plane before dinner. I tilt the glass, and then my conscience kicks in. Fuck it. I take a drink instead and reach down to scoop up a photo. That's when I choke on my ginger ale. I swear I've seen that girl somewhere before.

"Who's this?" I ask between coughs, holding up the picture.

"Damn it, Jacob. You're not supposed to touch that." Of course. I bite my lip. Here we go again.

I stare at the girl's face and feel another headache coming on. Why does she look familiar? "She been missing a long time?"

My mom rolls her eyes. "Jacob, that's the girl that we found on

6

Monday."

"Oh. You mean the dead one?"

"Yes. Samantha Young. She went to the high school you'll be attending. Remember? I told you this already. It's been all over the news."

I suppose that's why her face seems familiar. "Sounds like I shouldn't be going to school here. Kind of a dangerous place to live."

My mom rubs her face like she's trying to rub this case from her mind. Or more likely, having to deal with me. "If I thought it was dangerous, I'd be the first one to send you on a plane back to your dad's."

She didn't take the bait. Okay, then. "Good to know. What's for dinner?"

Three

OLIVIA

I hate waiting tables. My mom says that's great because it will give me an incentive to go to college. *Really, Mom? Couldn't you just let me complain?* At least this is the last day I'll have to do it for a while. My mom's all about summer jobs, but during the school year all she lets me do is babysit. It's slow today, which makes things worse, because hearing what seemed like Samantha's voice at her parents' house is the only thing I have to focus on. The words replay over and over in my mind. *Stop him.*

I'm not going to lie. The voice I heard yesterday freaked me out in a horrible, ugly, twisted way. Just thinking about it makes my heart pound. And pound. And pound. Because here's the thing. My dad heard voices too. And he had a diagnosis: schizophrenia.

One time when I was seven, I heard a voice that wasn't there. But that was one time. I read on the Internet that "otherwise healthy children sometimes start hearing voices after a traumatic experience." And that day, ten years ago, was one hell of a traumatic experience.

But that should have been it. One voice, one day. Over. Done.

You could say that the death of my friend last week was another traumatic experience.

That hearing her voice, if not exactly normal, was explainable.

But what if that's not the end of it? What if, instead of one voice on one day, I start to hear an explosion of voices? Voices that never stop. Voices that take over my life and rob me of everything normal.

What if I become my dad?

That thought makes me stop dead in the center of the aisle, a Mountain Dew in one hand, a hamburger platter in the other.

"Whoa, Olivia! Not funny!" James nearly crashes into me, a tray balanced on one palm above his head. He dodges, swooping around me. "What the hell?" he says.

"Sorry," I say. I don't try to explain.

I drop off the Mountain Dew and platter where they belong and go back to the kitchen for a glass of water and to clear my head.

The water hits the spot. I gulp it down. "Save some for the customers," teases Andrew, one of the cooks. He tosses the ingredients in his skillet into the air and they all fall neatly back into place.

"Nice," I say.

He smiles. Then a huge flame erupts from the pan, jumping into the air.

Fire.

The world moves in slow motion.

I lift my hands to cover my face, dropping my glass, which shatters on the ground.

I have to get out of here! We all have to get out of here! Why can't I move? Why can't I open my eyes?

"Hey there! Olivia! It's okay," says Andrew. "I got it under control. Happens a dozen times a day. You know that. It's all good. See? Look here."

9

I force myself to open my eyes. He's right. Of course he's right. *Way to overreact.*

I try to smile and stop my hands from shaking. "Yeah, I'm sorry. I feel like such an idiot. Let me get the broom."

"Oh, don't you worry about it. Dealing with all those customers is enough to make anyone a little jumpy. I'll get the broom. You go outside and get a little fresh air."

"Thanks, Andrew. You're an angel."

"Tell my wife that the next time you see her, will you?"

"Your wife adores you and you know it."

"Yeah, I know. Now go on outside. I'll cover for you."

Andrew holds the door open for me, squeezing my shoulder as I pass. I plop down on the bench outside and take in some deep breaths. *Get it together.*

Even though the view is somewhat obscured by the dumpster, the mountains in the distance do me good, and a few minutes later, while I'm not exactly Zen, I'm at least ready to go back to work.

Andrew pokes his head out the door. "Doing better?"

I nod.

"Good. Because James keeps jabbering about you needing to take an order for table five. You got it, or should I tell him to—"

"I got it. Thanks, Andrew."

Andrew holds the door open again and I weave my way through the kitchen, staying as far away from the burners as I can without being too obvious about it.

I head to table five with a glass of water in one hand and my order pad and pen in the other. I don't even try to do that memorization thing. People who can do that freak me out.

From a distance, the guy in the booth looks about my age, but I don't recognize him. Sandy hair. I can't tell the color of his eyes because he's bent over his phone, texting.

When I get to his table I set down the water and say, "Hi, my name's Olivia. I'll be your server."

He flips his phone over, picks up the silverware set, and pulls the paper wrapper off the napkin.

Then he looks up at me.

His eyes are green. And gorgeous.

Somehow his eyes go right from my face to my left arm. He sucks in his breath. Not too loud, but loud enough. And drops the silverware.

Typical. I roll my eyes and push my sleeve back down so it covers my scar.

We both bend down at the same time to pick up the silverware and bump heads. Great. I've just gone from embarrassed to mortified.

I grab the napkin. He hands me the spoon. The knife and fork are too far under the booth for me to reach. I'll get them later.

"I'm really sorry about that," he says. I know he's not talking about the silverware. "It's not what you—I mean, it's not—I wasn't—"

"Don't worry about it," I say. I've heard it all before. "Let me get you some clean ones." I take the dirty spoon to the bussing station and pick up another set of silverware.

Then I take a deep breath and try to pull myself together.

I know what my mom would say. *Any guy who only sees you for your scar isn't worth your time.*

Fine, Mom. But why does this one have to be so hot?

Four

JACOB

*E*ven though it's Sunday, my mom's working her case, so I cruise over to a diner in town for lunch. Half of the booths are red, the other half are yellow. And there's some weird geometric shapes in frames instead of actual pictures. Man, this place needs a makeover. I'm texting Ricky when a glass of ice water shows up next to my hand and the waitress starts introducing herself. I take the wrapper off the silverware set and look up.

Holy hell. That's not a waitress. That's got to be a model. But here she is with one of those order pads and a pen. I flip my phone over so she can't see the obscenities in Ricky's message.

Then I blow it.

There's this scar on her arm, and I get this frickin' sense of déjà vu. As if I've seen that scar before. I make some sort of sound and drop my silverware on the ground like a moron. Who *does* that shit?

She's pissed.

"I'll be right back," she says, taking off with the dirty spoon.

I lean under the table and grab the knife and fork and do some quiet drumming against the table. The napkin dispenser doubles as a decent cymbal in a pinch.

When the hot-as-fire waitress makes her way back with the new set of silverware, I quickly stash my contraband drumsticks next to me on the bench. "So what's there to do in this town?" I ask. Olivia, that's her name.

Her hair is dark and long and sort of wavy. It's pulled back, but a few ringlets have escaped and bounce in front of her ears. I want to bury my face in them. *If you hadn't blown this, maybe you could have.*

She taps her pen against the order pad. "Can I take your order?"

Wow. Complete shutdown. I guess I deserve it. "You have ginger ale?"

"Nope."

"Coke?"

"We have Pepsi." She sounds almost triumphant. Hey, if this makes up for the scar thing, I can drink Pepsi.

"Sold. How's the Reuben?"

"The pulled pork is better."

"Pulled pork it is, then." She reaches for the menu at the same time I start to hand it to her. Her fingers brush mine for just a second, and adrenaline zings through my veins. And then she's gone.

I do some more drumming to pass the time, then go wash my hands. On my way back to my table, I notice a flyer for a bike race on the bulletin board.

When Olivia returns with my order, I notice how long her legs are. And slender. And...

"Rock climbing, kayaking, and caving," she says, setting the plate down in front of me. I get a whiff of barbecue and honey, and my mouth starts to water.

"Excuse me?"

"You asked what there is to do in this town. I assume you're not interested in feeding ducks at the park or joining the garden club?"

"Right. I mean, no, I'm not. I take it you like the outdoors? Since that's what made your list of top attractions."

"Definitely."

"So maybe you'd be interested in that bike race. The one on the bulletin board over there."

"Oh yeah, that. It was ages ago. I forgot to take the flyer down. It was a blast. Did you want me to bring extra sauce?"

"No, I'm good."

"Enjoy your meal then," she says and saunters away, hips swaying, hair bouncing. Shit. Why didn't I ask for the sauce? It would have given her a reason to come back.

The sandwich is actually pretty good. I'm about halfway through it when Mom and Company come through the door. Great. She hasn't seen me yet. *Let's keep it that way.* I slump down in the booth, put on my Pink Floyd cap, and catch Olivia's attention as she walks by. "Could I get this to go, Olivia?" I ask.

She wrinkles her forehead and looks surprised that I remembered her name, but picks up my plate. "I'll put this in a box." As she comes back out of the kitchen, she points the doggy bag in my direction and tells my mom she'll be with them in a minute. I duck, pretending to look for my napkin.

Olivia brings me the bag and holds out the bill. I reach for it, and our fingers touch again, just a bit longer than the last time. A bit of color springs to her cheeks. "Have a nice day," she says, looking me straight in the eye.

"You too." I pause. "Olivia." We're still looking at each other, and it's almost a contest to see who's going to look away first.

"Miss?" Some asshole at another table is holding up his empty cup, and she's gone.

I open my wallet and leave more than enough to cover the check, then I slink over to the door before my mom can notice me. I sneak another look at Olivia's graceful silhouette. *Forget it, loser.* I stifle a sigh, head out the door, and drive my truck back home.

Five

JACOB

A fter my big strikeout at the restaurant, I head over to the gym. I get a lot of extra pull-ups in because every time I think of the girl at the restaurant—Olivia—I lose track of the count. And I think of her a lot.

By the time dinner rolls around, Mom's still not home. No big shocker. I chow down on a frozen pizza, then blast Aerosmith's *"Dream On,"* playing along on my drum set. I'm just waiting for the neighbors to complain, but not a peep. After that I FaceTime Ricky.

"Oh, that's right," he gloats. "You're off to school tomorrow."

"Oh, shut up. You're back in a week. I'll probably get off a week earlier in June."

"Yeah, but meanwhile, I'll be poolside tomorrow, knocking back some brew. And you'll be grinding out quadratic equations."

"Quadratic equations? I always knew you were a math nerd." Thing about Ricky is, he could totally be a math nerd if he weren't more interested in partying.

He ignores my comment. "So, is FBI mom gonna read you a bedtime story? One with knives and serial killers?"

"She's been AWOL all day, man."

"Hot damn! What are you doing talking to me? Go get you some mileage on that gift of mine. Find out where stuff's happening."

"Will do, Ricky. Go enjoy that pool you don't have."

"Didn't I tell you? Your dad invited me to hang out at his new place. Gonna take me out on the boat, let me drive the Corvette."

"In your dreams, you sick bastard."

After I hang up with Ricky, I take out his "gift" to me. A fake ID for Pennsylvania. Must have cost him a pretty penny, but he wouldn't take anything for it. I stare at it for a few minutes, deciding. Then I toss it in my desk drawer and grab my keys. Tonight I just want to drive.

I head outside, climb in my beat-up truck, and take her for a spin. I change the station because the one that's on is playing commercials. I'm not too picky about what kind of music I listen to, just as long as the drums are loud. After escaping the streets filled with Victorian houses and the old-fashioned downtown, I finally make it to the open road, where the fields rush by and the breeze slaps my face.

If I were writing the fictionalized movie version of my life, I'd change the part where my parents break up because of my brother's disappearance. That's the cliché version, after all. It started with a game of hide-and-seek, the second my dad and I closed our eyes. We never saw the bastard who took my brother. We never even knew he was missing until we couldn't find him in any of the usual places. Not until we called for him over and over again and he didn't answer. That was when I remembered hearing the squeal of tires in the parking lot while my eyes were clamped shut. They kept asking me if I knew what the car looked like, and I kept telling them no, but I knew what it sounded like. Wasn't that good enough?

No clue what it looks like when a family falls apart, but what it sounds like? Yeah, that I know. It's the squeal of tires in a parking lot, muffled sobs in the night, a phone that doesn't stop ringing, and then a phone that doesn't ring at all.

I think it's the silence that does it, really. It was the last breath of our dying family, the one that told us we were out of hope. My mother couldn't forgive us. Not that day, not any day. Not ever. I couldn't forgive her either. She was the FBI agent. Why the hell couldn't she find her own son?

Even though they were broken, my parents stayed together until I started seventh grade. They stayed in that same house, waiting for my brother to come back to us. They didn't keep his room as a shrine. No, they did what they were supposed to. They packed up all of his things and put them in the basement. Then my mom put a pink-and-white bedspread on the bed as if by changing the décor we could forget for even one second. My brother's bedroom became the guest room we never needed because no one ever came to visit because we never asked them to.

And then my mom decided that we should move. To someplace close enough that she could keep her job at the FBI field office in Pittsburgh, but far enough that she could stop driving past that park every day. My dad decided that we should move too—only, his solution was eight hundred miles away. My parents told me I could decide where I wanted to live, and I chose my dad, expecting my mom to fight for me. Only she never did. That's how I ended up spending the past four years speaking to her only on Sundays, except for a week at Christmas and two in the summer. That's when she would take me on a vacation. Luckily we were always doing so much we didn't have time to talk about anything that actually mattered.

I cruise around for a while until I need to stop for gas, then I fill up and reluctantly head back toward home. I'm jamming along to the radio, just chillin', when a stabbing pain hits me right between the temples. Even though it's past dinnertime, the sunlight seems blinding, and I have to slip on a pair of shades. I see a dirt road up ahead and take it, then I pull off to the side. I put the truck in park, turn it off, and close my eyes to block out the knife blades hacking away at my forehead.

When I open them again, I'm lying on the bench seat, and it's beyond dark. What time is it? Ten-thirty. *Ten-thirty?* Can you black out from a headache? 'Cause that was no nap. I still feel like shit. I vigorously rub my head. *Damn. Is that a cut?* What a dumbass. I must have whacked my head against the radio on my way to not-so-pleasant dreamsville. I root around in the glove compartment. When I find a bottle with the words "pain reliever" on it, I pop three of those suckers in and swallow. I start the truck, leaving the bottle open in the cup holder, just in case, and backtrack to the main drag. When I get back, my mom is probably going to freak out about my not getting enough sleep before the first day of school. At least I shouldn't be that far away. A mile or so down the road I get my answer. End Essex City Limits. Ridgeview 10.

The only time I've been to Ridgeview High was to pick out my schedule. That was enough. I still can't believe that my mom expects me to start my junior year at a new school. With the hours my mom has been putting in on this case, I'll have even less supervision here than I did at my dad's house. So what's the point?

When I pull up in front of our house, the whole place is dark. Inside, I realize my mom isn't even home yet. So much for the back-to-school lecture. So much for anyone caring that my headaches are getting worse instead of better.

I sit down on the couch, leaving the lights off. What am I even doing here? My mom and me, this is so fucking not going to work. I know my mom's hunting down serial killers. I know that by working this late, she's going to stop some psycho from killing other girls. I'm a total dickhead for being annoyed about her not being home, but... Jesus, will someone tell me why no one worked this hard to stop the psycho who took *my* brother before he ripped *our* family apart? And why they still haven't found him...or my brother? Just tell me that, and I'll shut the hell up.

Six

JACOB

*he fucking dream always starts the same way. Tonight is no different. I'm high on a ledge in a place that looks like the Grand Canyon. I'm alone. I put my arms out to my sides, and I fly. It's easy. It feels natural. Peaceful. Then I see the other side of the cliff. I try to stay away, but the wind keeps pulling me in that direction. People are lined up there several rows deep, side by side, their toes at the edge of the cliff.

"Don't do it!" I shout. "Stay where you are!"

A girl jumps.

No matter what I say, someone always jumps.

And I always get sucked down with them.

This one is about my age. Dark blond hair. Blue eyes. Freckles. A cute nose. Jeans. Baby blue sweater. Hoop earrings. Dolphin necklace.

We fall for a long time. I reach my hand out, and for a minute our fingers touch. I squeeze as hard as I can, but her hand slips out of mine.

"Put your arms out like this!" I shout.

She puts them out, but it doesn't do any good. It never does.

I stop falling. I'm able to fly again, so I head back up to the top of the cliff.

She doesn't. Her body slams into the ground.

I wake up and turn on the light. Sweat trickles into my ears.

Fuck this shit.

I fumble in my nightstand, yanking out a sketchbook and a pencil, my heart pounding something fierce.

Bam! Instant replay on a continual loop in my mind.

I flip to a blank page. Her face. *Think!* Long hair, oval eyes. No, they were narrower. More like this.

Bam!

Damn it, hand, stop shaking! I flick my wrist in the air. *Get in line! Work!*

Bam!

I sketch furiously, choking on the details, her face fading fast in my mind. Necklace. Dolphin necklace. Like that? I don't know.

Did I get it right? Any of it?

Bam!

I throw the pencil across the room.

What does it matter anyway, you moron? It's just a dream.

At least my hand stops shaking. I take a deep breath.

Better. That feels better.

I flip back a few pages. Another night. Another dream. Another girl's face.

I snap my fingers. The girl in the file. I tilt the page. Maybe...

A fluke probably. I grab my phone and search up the Sweet Dreams Strangler.

There's the girl. Samantha Young. I check the date she was reported missing and the date she was found. One day in between.

There you have it. I drew the picture in between the two. Obviously, I must have seen some sort of news coverage the day she disappeared.

I look over at my nightstand and see a cup full of pencils, courtesy of my mom. I snort. She may have screwed up a lot of things, but she does manage to get some things exactly right. I grab another pencil and scrawl Samantha's name at the bottom of the page.

Samantha girl, a lot of people here must be missing you. My mom never found the piece of shit who took my brother. But I'm fucking sure she's going to find the one who killed you.

Seven

JACOB

"*G*et up, it's time for school," says my mom, her voice all peppy.
"Ha, very funny," I say, rolling over and pulling the blankets over my head to block out the light.

My mom yanks them right back off. "Not kidding." She stares down at me, a towel wrapped around her head.

"I've changed my mind. I know I said I would be okay living here with you, but I'm not. I want to go back to Michigan. So there's no point in my starting school here." I pull the covers back over my head.

"We've been through this, Jacob. Your dad's entering a new phase in his life and—"

I turn on my side. "And I need to get the fuck out of it."

"Watch the language, Jacob." I can hear her opening the blinds. "By the way, don't make plans for Friday. We're picking up your new car that day."

"Car? What car?" I peek out from under the covers. Then I return to reality. "There's no way you'd let me have a new car."

24

"It's for your birthday."

I sit up. "Why would you let me have a new car after all that shit with Ricky?"

"You weren't driving."

"Yeah, but I was drinking."

"Which you won't be doing anymore."

"Arc you going to stop me?"

"No, Jacob, you are going to stop you. With the help of a counselor if you want."

I laugh. "That's not how it works, you know. That's not how you fix your out-of-control teen. You don't start off trusting he's going to do the right thing. You just flunked teen parenting 101 right there."

"Just how did you expect this to work? I make up a lot of rules, you break them, and then I give up on you and send you back to your dad? Sound about right?"

I snort. "That sounds exactly right."

"I'm sorry you think I don't love you, Jacob, but I do. Let's try this: I'll trust you not to break any local or state laws for the next month, and if you can manage that, at the end of the month you can choose where you want to live. And if you choose to live with your dad, you can take the car with you."

"That sounds a lot like—"

"Like bribery? Yeah, I know."

"It's not going to work, you know."

"It's a red Mustang. Brand new."

"You can't afford it."

"Your dad's paying for it."

Well, there you go. Now it all makes sense. My dad is bribing me into staying here so he can have a new life with his brand-new wife. Fine, Dad. You don't want me, I don't need you.

"Of course they'll impound the car if you get picked up for a DUI."

25

I don't know what head games my parents are trying to play with me. All I know is, right now all I want to do is take that car and drive it right over that cliff in my dream.

My mood doesn't improve as I shower and then throw on a pair of jeans and a Grateful Dead T-shirt. By the time I'm ready, my mom has already left. I get in the truck and turn the key. Nothing. I try again. *Shit.* The battery's dead. Just my luck. I thunk my head against the steering wheel and contemplate going back inside and vegging out on the couch all day. Then I think about the girl at the restaurant yesterday. Olivia. I wonder if she goes to the same school as me and if we'll have any classes together. What the hell. I get out of the truck, slam the door, and start walking.

Eight

OLIVIA

⟨ornament⟩

*W*hen I get to chemistry, HE is there. The guy from the restaurant. Mr. I've-Never-Seen-a-Scar-Before. And the only open seat is right in front of him. It's obvious he recognizes me, and this sly, sort of sexy smile takes over his face.

"Hi, Olivia," he says. His voice is raspy. I try to hate him, but instead I feel all fluttery inside. At least he has the good sense not to look at my arm again. Which is actually going to be pretty awkward for him. I'm going to have fun seeing how long this will last.

"Thought you were just passing through," I say.

"No such luck. But at least I know someone here." He tilts his chin. Crap. He's just as cute from that angle.

"You mean me?" *Real smooth, Olivia.*

He stares at me, not answering. I stare back, taking note of the chocolaty flecks in his green eyes.

"What's your name?" I ask.

"Jacob."

I rip my eyes away from his and try to shake off the hold he seems to have over me.

"So where are you from?"

He looks around, everywhere except my scar. "I used to live kind of nearby. Then I moved with my dad to northern Michigan—the Upper Peninsula. But my dad got remarried. So now I live with my mom. She's an FBI agent. Sorry, I don't know why I said that. Except that I know you guys just lost someone, and from all the long faces, I'm guessing she was pretty special."

My throat tightens, and all I can do is nod.

"Sorry for your loss."

"Thanks," I say. I clear my throat. "Northern Michigan. It must be beautiful there. Have you seen the Northern Lights?"

"A few times."

"I'm jealous."

"Okay, folks, let's get started," says Mr. Fredericks. He hands copies of the syllabus to the first person in each row. When the papers get to me, I take one and pass the rest back to Jacob.

Mr. Fredericks begins his ramble on classroom expectations. As he drones on, the temperature in the room plummets. They really need to do a better job of regulating the air conditioning in this school. Talk about waste. I rub my bare arms, trying to warm them up.

"You cold?" whispers Jacob.

I turn partway in my seat. "Yeah, it's freezing in here."

"You want my jacket? I haven't figured out where my locker is yet, so I brought it with me."

At this point I'm so cold I don't care what anyone thinks about me wearing the new guy's jacket. "Please."

As Jacob reaches for his jacket, someone whispers my name.

I look around.

Olivia!

There it is again. Damn it! Not now!

It's Samantha's voice, and it seems to be coming from Jacob's desk.

I look underneath his desk, just to make sure someone's not down there messing with me.

"You drop your pencil or something?" Jacob asks.

I shake my head.

Olivia! It's Samantha again. And sure enough, her voice sounds like it's coming from Jacob's notes. Great. He hasn't written much down, except for a whole lot of doodles of dolphins.

I take the jacket from Jacob and slip it on. "Thanks," I say.

Olivia! Look!

Not real. I pinch my ears shut with my index fingers. It's fairly discrete. If anyone is watching, they'll think I'm trying to drown out Mr. Fredericks. But it doesn't do any good. I cover both ears completely with my hands. If I'm lucky, Mr. Fredericks will think I'm propping my head up so I don't fall asleep. It doesn't work. Of course not. Since the voice is in my head.

Do not talk to me, Samantha. You aren't real. You're dead. Therefore, you can't talk to me. It's not possible. If you try to talk to me, I'm not going to listen.

It's getting harder and harder to ignore her because she's shouting now.

Olivia!

Nine

JACOB

*t's hard not to stare at Olivia. She *is* sitting in front of me. And she's wearing my jacket. Though I don't know how she could possibly be cold. It's baking up in here. I don't buy that she was just angling to wear my jacket. She doesn't seem the type. She keeps covering her ears. First one, then the other, then both. I'm not sure if she's trying to drown out the lecture or if it's a not-so-subtle hint that she doesn't want to talk to me anymore. Five minutes before the class is over, Mr. Fredericks finishes his droning. Olivia puts her head down. It's probably better that she hasn't turned around since I've been drawing dolphins all over my paper for the last hour. Not exactly macho. I shove the paper into my binder, then grab a couple of pencils, give them a good twirl, and tap out a rhythm on the back of Olivia's chair. No reaction from her, not even a swat or a "cut it out."

The guy sitting next to me says, "Hey, man. You play?"

"Sure do," I say. "I mean, I'm not into the whole marching band scene, but I used to play in a band before I moved here. Probably the worst thing about leaving."

"I hear you. A few of us are in a band, and our drummer just quit on us. You interested?"

"You play country, I take it," I say, nodding at his T-shirt. It says, "If it ain't country, it ain't music."

"You got it. I'm Nick, by the way."

Country's not my usual thing, but what the heck? It beats hanging around an empty house. "I'm Jacob. Sure, I can help you out. See how it goes," I say.

"Awesome." We do a half-slap, half-handshake. "Let me get your number. We practice tomorrow."

Olivia sits up and turns around. She takes off my jacket and hands it to me. "Thanks a lot." As she leans closer, I catch a whiff of lilacs.

"No problem. You can keep it for a while if you're still cold."

She looks uncertain. "No, I think I'll be okay," she says. "All of a sudden I feel a lot warmer."

Ten

JACOB

When school gets out, I join the mob rushing the doors. Most head for the parking lot. All except for us fitness geeks (aka losers without cars) who start trudging home on foot. The crowd thins out. Surprisingly, I recognize two of my fellow walkers. One, a girl from my English class, is wearing a white shirt with multicolored polka dots, like someone threw a bowl of wet M&M's at her. The other has soft flowing hair and a skirt that swishes. Olivia. I run and catch up with her.

"You live this way?" I ask, falling into step next to her. *Duh.*

She stops for a second and shakes her head. "You just scared the hell out of me."

"Sorry."

"It's okay. So how do you like Ridgeville?"

"Most of the classes were pretty uninspiring.   But there was one—chemistry—that I think has some potential."

A smile tugs at her lips. "Does it now?"

As we pass a yellow ranch with a white picket fence, a fierce-looking dog runs alongside us, barking like crazy. Olivia doesn't even look over at him. "He does this every day," she says. "You'd think he'd give up by now."

"Maybe he's trying to communicate with you. Maybe he's hoping every day that you'll understand and talk back."

Olivia freezes and looks at me funny. Only it's not a "you've got to be crazy" look or even a "not funny" look. It's something else, I'm just not quite sure what.

"Sorry," I say quickly, shouting over the barking. "I was just kidding."

"Right." The look disappears from her face, but her forehead remains crinkled. We keep walking.

"So what's the homework for chemistry again?"

She shakes her head. "There wasn't any."

"I guess that explains why I don't have anything written in my notes."

"Does it?" Olivia raises one eyebrow.

I have no idea how to read that. There's an awkward silence.

At the stop sign, she pauses. "I'm going this way."

My mom's house is in the opposite direction. "I'm the other way. So I guess I'll see you tomorrow," I say.

"Yeah. See you," she says, turning away.

"Unless..."

"Unless what?" she says, sounding suspicious.

"Well, since there's no homework, you want to go do something?"

"I don't know. We just met today."

"Actually, it was yesterday. We met yesterday."

"Right. At the restaurant." Her voice is strained. Why do I keep reminding her about my gawking?

"It's just that—well, you're the only person I know." Except for Nick and some guys from my history class who invited me to sit with them at lunch. But I keep that little tidbit to myself.

"I actually have some homework already."

"Me too. But we could still grab something to eat."

"I kind of get enough of restaurants from my summer job."

"Anywhere you want then. My treat." *Way to sound desperate, Jacob.*

"Anywhere?"

"Uh, yeah. Anywhere." This time I put a little less enthusiasm into my "anywhere." I imagine the possibilities. I brace myself for the words, "Let's go shopping." Instead she says, "Let's play laser tag."

I really need to get my hearing checked. "It sounded like you just said, 'let's play laser tag.'"

"I did," she answers. "Unless you'd rather go shopping."

"No, no. Laser tag is great. Perfect."

"Okay then. Let me give you my address."

Address? Oh yeah, right. "There's just one thing," I say.

"What's that?" She narrows her eyes at me.

"Any way you could drive? I mean, I have a truck, but the battery's dead. If you want to give me a jump, I'd be happy to drive. Or I can drive your parents' car if you want," I say obligingly.

She snorts. "No chance of that. I've got my own car. I just like to walk when the weather's nice. Where do you live?"

Eleven

OLIVIA

*A*t home I run up the stairs to my room and change, way overthinking my choice. Mammoth Cave T-shirt? Too faded. Burgundy top? Too wrinkled. *Get it together, Olivia.* I finally settle for a long-sleeved green top and a pair of sparkly earrings. I trot down the stairs, grab my keys off the hook, and poke my head in the living room. My mom is home since she doesn't teach afternoon classes at the college.

"I'm headed out to laser tag," I say and aim for the door.

"Hold on there," says my mom.

I swing back around, my hand still on the doorknob.

"What about your homework?"

"There's hardly any homework on the first day."

"Who's all going?"

Somehow "A hot guy you've never met who needs me to pick him up" doesn't sound so good. I improvise. "Some of us from the Outdoor Adventure Club." *Shit. Why did I lie like that? Well, maybe Jacob will join.*

He seems the type. Well, he could be the type.

"Isn't laser tag indoors?"

"Yeah, but it's kind of like paintball, and that's outdoors."

"I don't think…"

"I'll text you once I'm there." I don't wait for her to reply. "See you, Mom!" I say, and slip out the door.

Just exactly what are you doing, Olivia? Despite his faux pas with the scar, I'm definitely attracted to Jacob. But how will he react when he learns that bird figurines and random pieces of paper are trying to talk to me?

When I get to his house, Jacob is relaxing on his front porch in a Detroit Pistons T-shirt that shows off his chiseled arms. As I pull my Jeep into the driveway, he looks up and breaks into a grin.

He opens the car door and gets in. "Awesome ride," he said. "Sure you don't need me to drive?"

"Definitely not," I say. "But you better buckle up. I've been known to take corners a little fast."

"So you must make pretty good tips at the restaurant." He rubs his hand across the dashboard and pats the glove box.

"Definitely not. This was my mom's lease car. When the lease expired, she was so many miles over, I convinced her to pass it on to me at a considerable discount. She wanted a minivan so she could take our bikes places without a bike rack. It helped that I said she could still have visitation rights."

"Visitation rights? Does that include driving rights?"

"Sometimes."

"Is there any way other people can get visitation rights for her?"

"*Her*, huh? Forget it. Moving on to more important questions."

Whoops. There's the Arby's. I'm supposed to turn. I squeeze my way into the left-turn lane and slide through the light as it changes from yellow to red. The tires squeal just a tiny bit, and Jacob grabs the handle on the door.

Twelve

JACOB

"More important questions?" I say, trying not to cringe as oncoming traffic nearly clips us as we make a left.

"Uh-huh," she says. "Like, is your battery really dead, or did someone dare you to ride in a car with me?"

What the hell? "Why would someone dare me to ride with you?"

"Oh, no reason." She puts on an innocent face.

"Right. Not buying it. Spill."

She shrugs and shakes the hair tumbling over her shoulders. "Let's just say my ex and off-roading weren't a good mix. What's your stance on mud?"

"A little dirt never hurt?"

Her bright blue eyes light up. "Thank you." She guns the gas pedal, speeding through the intersection. "I mean, who wears designer jeans and Nikes off-roading? And it's not like it took us all day to walk back to civilization. It was two hours, max."

"Huh, I heard it was three and a half, and the mud was waist high."

"Three and the mud only came to our knees. Well, Simon is kind of short. Maybe to him it seemed higher."

I laugh. "Simon, huh?"

"What do you mean? Who told you?" A tiny furrow pops up on her forehead.

"Nobody. Besides you, that is. But it's good to know who to thank."

"What are you talking about? Thank for what?"

"For being a wimp. I'm guessing that's why you're single?"

"You got that right. But you better watch it. If you try tricking me like that again, I can't guarantee how smooth my next turn will be." She laughs.

"Scouts honor. I don't want a repeat of that last left."

She pretends to pout. "Come on, it wasn't that bad."

I clear my throat.

"Okay, so it *was* that bad." She flicks on the turn signal. "See how I'm signaling now? I'm going to make a nice, calm turn into the parking lot."

I glance over at her arm on the steering wheel and think about the scar underneath her sleeve. How did she get it? I don't dare ask. I'd probably end up insulting her. The sense of déjà vu I had at the restaurant starts to bother me again. Where have I seen a scar like that before? But the harder I think, the fuzzier the memory becomes, and the more I just want to be around to protect her from any more bad shit. Okay, never mind the bad shit. I just want to be around her.

"I know you love this Jeep, but we're here." The engine is off, and Olivia's holding the keys in her hand.

I shake my head, focusing on the here and now. "Right," I say and open the car door.

Thirteen

OLIVIA

he asphalt in the parking lot is crumbling, and I stumble a
bit on one of the rough edges. Jacob grabs my arm, and an
electric spark runs through me.

"This parking lot could use some work," says Jacob. "Make that a lot
of work. And what's with the sign? What's 'Lase ap'? Phone games for
lazy people?"

"It's Laser Zap. And yeah, the building's seen better days. But they
redid the inside, and that's all that matters."

"If you say so," Jacob says, raising his eyebrows. He holds the door,
and we get in line to pay. I recognize the girl working the counter
with her purple hair and nose ring. Rebecca. She points at me and
says, "Oh hey, Olivia. You want to be Warrior Princess again today?"

Jacob bursts out laughing. I nod. "Make him Thor," I say.

He stops laughing. "Hold on! Thor? Let me change that," he says.

"Oh, sorry," Rebecca says. "It's already in the computer." She
shrugs at him. Jacob rolls his eyes, pulls out his wallet, and holds

out a twenty. Rebecca hands him his change and two green Mardi Gras–style necklaces.

He waves them off. "No, thanks."

"They're to show we paid," I say, taking them from Rebecca. I put one on and drop the other over Jacob's head. "The waiting area is this way."

Jacob follows me over to a group of benches, then folds his arms and frowns at me.

"Thor? Really?"

"Teach you to make fun of the Warrior Princess."

"I take it you come here a lot," he says. "Since that girl knows your name and this isn't even the town you go to school in."

"You mean that *we* go to school in. You and I now attend the same high school, in case you've forgotten."

"Don't try to change the subject."

"Okay, I come here a lot. So?"

"So it's pretty cool, that's what. A girl who drives a Jeep and plays laser tag."

I shake my head. "Oh no, not just plays. Who *rules* at laser tag. You better watch it in there. I can be pretty wicked."

He nods and looks around the waiting area. A bunch of ten-year-old boys are playing Pac-Man.

"Okay, so the competition isn't that fierce," I say. "Except when we come with the Outdoor Adventure Club."

"*Outdoor* Adventure Club?"

"Yeah, well, you try picking something to do outdoors when it's five below."

I sit down on the wooden bench. Jacob sits next to me, closer than he needs to. His leg brushes mine, and little tingles radiate across my skin.

"So what actual outdoor activities does the club do?"

41

"Mountain biking, cross-country skiing, snowboarding, paintball, caving."

"Caving?"

"Yeah, you know. Spelunking. Tromping around in caves."

Jacob makes a face.

"What? You don't like spelunking?" I ask.

"I'm not really fond of dark, drippy places inhabited by bats."

"You're afraid of bats?"

"That's not what I said."

"Funny, that's what I heard. Well, too bad. Since that's what we're doing next meeting. This Saturday, in fact."

He pulls the bead necklace over his head and starts swinging it like a lasso. "Hmm. In that case, I suppose I could put aside my dislike for bats."

"Just so you know, we're not doing the standard tour. We're doing the hard-core crawling-through-tunnels, dirt-underneath-the-fingernails version. You're not claustrophobic, are you?"

"Nah. How do I sign up?"

"Mr. Cushing is the club sponsor. You can talk to him."

Jacob shrugs his shoulders.

"Bio and zoology teacher. First floor. His room is near the library. Just ask around. Or...I could show you his room after chemistry tomorrow."

"That'd be great. Thanks." The beads fly out of his hand and land partway across the room. Jacob goes over and scoops them up.

The girl behind the counter gets on the microphone. You can barely hear her over the blaring music. God, as much as I love laser tag, I'd hate to work here. "Players, please proceed to the gaming area."

We line up with the ten-year-olds and a group of high school students who appear from the party room. Although they're not from my school, I recognize a few Laser Zap regulars and nod a greeting, which sets

Jacob off on another laughing trip. I elbow him in the ribs.

The door to the game area opens like an elevator in *Star Trek*. We enter and put on our gear. As we're let loose in the gaming area, I turn toward Jacob to warn him not to expect any special treatment from me, but he's already gone. I go into stealth mode and make my way through the dark, tagging a few easy targets as I hunt for Jacob. *This guy's better at this than he let on.* I turn each corner, expecting him to be there waiting for me.

That's when it starts. Suddenly the room is ice-cold. I rub my arms, but it doesn't help in the least. One of the ten-year-olds nearly tags me.

My teeth chatter. I just want to get warm again. I run to get my circulation going. After this game, I'm going to grab a coffee. I don't drink coffee, but I'm going to get one anyhow. Some really hot stuff. I'll sit with my hands over the cup and let the steam work its magic.

My ears are ringing, ringing, ringing. I grunt in frustration. Then the chatter starts, like that commercial they play at the movie theater to get you to shut up. The one filled with all that mindless chatter and babies crying. Except there are no babies crying. I guess I should be glad about that, but I'm not.

Samantha's voice. She's shouting again. From the papier-mâché rocks at Laser Zap. Goddamn f-ing hell.

Olivia.

My arms go slack, and my laser gun drops to my side. When I can move my arms again, I cover my ears, but it doesn't do any good.

Olivia. There's not much time.

"Time? What do you mean, time?"

Damn it. Do not engage with the voice in the wall. It isn't real.

Suddenly Jacob is in front of me, his gun aimed straight at my heart, a grin on his face. He aims, fires, and my vest lights up.

Time. Not much time.

I feel like all of the air has been sucked out of me, and I crumple to the floor.

Jacob is next to me in an instant.

"Olivia?" he says. "Are you okay?"

I force myself to smile. "Just messing with you," I say weakly, clinging to him as he pulls me to my feet.

He lets go of me once I'm standing. I lean against the wall.

"Let's see what you've got then," he says, and he takes off.

"Don't go," I say.

But it's too late.

Fourteen

JACOB

⁓◦⦿⦿◦⁓

"*L*ooks like I blew you way out of the water," I say. "Game champion standing right here in front of you. Feel free to bow down."

Olivia rolls her eyes and winces. "Beginner's luck," she says.

"Hey, what makes you think I'm a beginner?"

"You just gave it away. Now get in before I change my mind and make you walk." By the time she gets to the end of her sentence, she seems out of breath and the word "walk" is barely above a whisper. She may have the same sassy attitude that she did when we got here, but she's pale as hell.

"You doing okay?" I ask. "Sure you didn't crack a rib when you fell?" She looks scared for a moment. What is she not telling me?

Then she pulls herself together. "Please," she says sarcastically. "Don't be ridiculous." Olivia opens her door and gets in the Jeep.

After she starts the car, I open the window to let in some air. Olivia starts to turn her head, then stops and checks the mirror instead.

"Anything behind us?"

I turn and look. "Nope—" Before I can add "all clear," Olivia guns the engine and whips out of the space.

As we head down the road, Olivia points out the landmarks she thinks will be of use to me. "This place has the best burgers," she says, gesturing to a red building called the Burger Barn. "Over there, you've got a decent bike shop. This movie theater is good if you're a bit strapped for cash. But if you want a better selection, the one in Stanton is the way to go."

"Thanks. I'll try to remember all that. Sounds like you still get out a lot, even with working at the…"

The restaurant. God. Why do I keep bringing up the restaurant?

"I don't work there during the school year. Just in summer. You came in during my last shift."

I take a deep breath. "You know, I just wanted to say that I'm sorry. About the restaurant. If it seemed like I was staring at your scar. I mean, I know I was staring. But not because it freaked me out or anything. It's just that I felt like I had seen that same scar before. It was like déjà vu. I know that sounds weird and all," I finish lamely.

"You're right. It does sound weird. But…" She sighs. "Apology accepted." She looks away. "I was seven. My…"

But she never finishes her sentence because all of a sudden there's a siren behind us. Cops.

Fifteen

OLIVIA

⚓

"No no no no no! Damn it!" I hit the steering wheel, and the horn sounds. I look down at the speedometer. "But I'm not even speeding. Really. Look!" I say to Jacob.

Could this day get any worse? Ever since I heard that voice at Laser Zap, I've felt like shit. It's hard to breathe, my whole body aches, and it hurts to turn my head. And to top it all off, now I'm being pulled over.

"Someone probably saw you back out of that parking space," Jacob mutters.

When I put my window down for the police officer, I panic and blurt out, "But I wasn't speeding."

"Are you Olivia Anderson?"

"Yes, but I wasn't speeding. I swear. Really, you can ask him." I point to Jacob, who obligingly says, "She wasn't."

"License and registration please."

As I hand it over, I realize that the police officer said my name before I gave him my ID. "Um, how did you know my name?"

The officer lifts his cap off his head and sighs. "Your mother. She reported you missing."

"Missing? But I've only been gone…" I look over at Jacob. "What? Two hours." I picture my mom sitting in the living room, where she was when I left the house. "Crap! I promised to text her from Laser Zap." I reach for my cellphone with one hand and cover my mouth with the other. "Sorry for swearing." I try to wake up my phone. Nothing. "I guess I forgot to charge it." I turn to Jacob. "Can I borrow yours?"

"Sure," he says, reaching into his pocket.

The officer hands me back my registration and ID, and for a minute he doesn't say anything. He readjusts his hat and looks off in the distance.

"You're going to want to call your mom right away." He clears his throat and bends down so he's looking me right in the eye. "They found another girl. Strangled. It's all over the news."

Sixteen

JACOB

I've got the radio tuned to a country station, trying to get a feel for the type of music played by the band I've promised to join, and I'm tapping out beats on the kitchen table when my dad calls.

"So what's the urgent message all about?" he says. "I've been out of the country. It was hard to call."

"Right. I'm sure Sophie made sure of that."

"Sophia. Stop pretending you don't know her name. We've been together for almost a year now. And we're married. It's getting ridiculous."

"I'll say," I mutter.

"So now you're mad at me? After you got into a car with that drunk?" The pitch of his voice skyrockets. He sighs. "What did you call about, Jacob? What do you want?"

I want you to care more about me than you do Sophia. But I don't say that. I just go silent. Which of course he can't stand.

I think about how pissed I was that my mom made me come live with her. How I miss the way things used to be with my dad. Playing basketball together. Going fishing. Watching R-rated movies.

And then I realize that my mom's too busy worrying about the case to keep close tabs on me. There's a new band. There's Olivia. And with my dad I'd just be in the way.

"Nothing," I say, resigned but not completely unhappy. "I don't want anything at all from you." And though it makes me feel like the shit that I am, I hang up.

I feel like breaking something. The closest thing is a butter dish. I wind up, but before I can pitch it, the lid comes free, and a blob of butter sticks to my hand, reminding me how much of a mess this will be if it ends up on the floor. So I set it down a bit forcefully on the table and grab a paper towel. I root around in the fridge. Still no beer. Not even a wine cooler. Same thing for the pantry. I settle for some Airheads and don't know whether to feel nostalgic or pissed that my mom is still shopping for me as if I were ten. I stuff one in my mouth. The sugar rush is as powerful as ever. I flop down on the couch and flip on the TV.

A reporter, looking miserable in the rain, appears on the screen. "This is the scene where the latest victim of the Sweet Dreams Strangler was found just hours ago."

"Seventeen-year-old Courtney Walker was found here, her body abandoned in a field sometime last night. Like the other victims of the Sweet Dreams Strangler, Walker's body was found wearing what is described to be an elegant dress. It's not what the victim was reported to have been wearing when she disappeared. Hair neatly combed, head resting on a pillow, and a blanket pulled up to her chin. Sources close to the investigation say that strangulation is the most likely cause of death."

They flash a picture of a girl in a "Save the Dolphins" T-shirt. It hits me like a kick to the gut.

Bam!

Long, dark blond hair. Blue eyes. Freckles. A cute nose.

Bam!

No. It's not. It couldn't be. I go grab the sketchpad off my nightstand anyway.

Bam!

By the time I get back to the living room, the news reporter has moved on, so I find the news coverage on my phone.

Courtney Walker.

My eyes dart back and forth between the photo online and the sketch I made in the middle of the night of the girl with the dolphin necklace.

Bam!

No. *Shake it off. Not possible.*

Freckles. I missed the freckles. *See, it's not the same girl.*

Bam!

It's not!

I can't do this. I shut the sketchbook and close the tab on my phone.

Even though this Courtney couldn't possibly be the girl I drew, she was someone's daughter, maybe even someone's sister. The ache of losing my own brother bubbles up inside me. It makes me want to pick up the phone and call my dad back. Say I'm sorry. I scroll through my contacts and bring up his number. My finger hovers over the phone icon.

Then I think about our phone call, and I know he won't even care. Good thing Olivia helped jump my battery before she left.

Stuffing my phone back into my pocket, I go to my room and grab Ricky's gift out of my drawer. Then I get in my truck and drive somewhere I can use it.

51

Seventeen

JACOB

⁓⧫⧫⧫⁓

"So how was your mom when you got home yesterday?" I ask Olivia as she sets up the test tubes we need for our chemistry lab. "Are you grounded forever?"

"Even she admitted that she overreacted by calling the cops. So no, I'm not on lockdown. How many drops of this do we need?"

I check the lab sheet. "Two."

"You know, Essex is west of here." She adds the two drops to the first test tube. As soon as they hit the rock at the bottom of the tube, it starts fizzing.

"Cool," I say. Olivia looks surprised. "About the fizzing." I shake my head. "Okay, so Essex is west of here. I think I'm missing something."

"I guess you haven't been following the news." Still holding the chemical in one hand and the dropper in the other, Olivia tries to push her goggles up higher with her arm. "The girl they found? Apparently she went missing the day before school started, but everyone thought she was a runaway. Up until now the Sweet Dreams Strangler has been moving east. And everyone assumed that he would keep moving in that direction. Now that he's switched things up, it's gotten people a bit on edge."

Essex. Now why does that name sound familiar?

Olivia fiddles with her goggles again. "These darn things never stay up."

"Here, let me help." I stand behind her and try to tighten the strap on her goggles.

Essex. Right. A sign. End of Essex city limits. The sign I saw right before I pulled over because of that headache. The day before school started. The day that girl went missing.

"Maybe you've been there? To Essex, I mean. There's a great pizza place there? Right on Main?"

My hand goes automatically to the cut above my eyebrow. "No, never been there," I lie. "Probably just sounds like a town back in Michigan."

Why did I just lie?

I know why. And it's stupid. Totally insane. I mean, sure, I've been a little angry lately, but obviously I wouldn't have killed some random stranger. Even if I can't account for all those hours I spent passed out in my truck the night she died.

What the fuck is wrong with me? Did I actually for a millisecond think I killed someone without even knowing it? Or saw a murder and blocked it out? Shit—between the headaches and the dreams, I feel like I'm losing my mind. Not only that, now I'm lying to the only person who makes me feel sane.

Samantha and Courtney were victims of a serial killer, plain and simple. The same guy who killed three girls in Ohio. Before the car wreck. Before the god-awful headaches. While I still lived in Michigan.

There's just one thing that still bothers me. The night that Olivia's friend Samantha died...I can't remember a thing about that night.

Except that my mom was out and I went to bed early because of a headache.

And that when I woke up, I was drawing her face.

Eighteen

OLIVIA

*In zoology the topic is birds. Okay, yes, I get that we should study birds in zoology class, but seriously, does it have to be now? Mr. Cushing keeps going through pictures of birds. Bluebirds. Hummingbirds. Owls. Goldfinches. Pigeons. Pigeons? Why are we looking at pigeons? Every time a bird flashes up on the screen, I wince. I keep thinking about the bird figurine at Samantha's house. I keep waiting for voices to come spewing out of their beaks. But none do.

After zoology, Mr. Cushing calls me over to his desk. He must have noticed all of my wincing and shifting in my seat. Maybe I should drop this class. He clears his throat. "As you know, there's an opening on Student Council now that Samantha's no longer...well, given the circumstances, we aren't going to hold elections just yet, but we need someone to fill her spot temporarily. Your name came up in some of the discussions."

So this doesn't have anything to do with my about-to-puke look during the entire class? My name came up for Student Council? It's *so* not my thing. Though it's hard to know how many of the girls who are on Student Council are doing it for the leadership experience and how many just want to hang around with Mr. Cushing, hot young teacher and faculty sponsor.

"Thanks for asking, Mr. Cushing. I'll think about it and get back to you."

"You do that," he says and waves at me as I leave the room. In the hall, I pull out my phone and call my contact for the field trip this Saturday.

"Hi, Kevin? This is Olivia Anderson, from the Ridgeview High School Outdoor Adventure Club?"

"Right. What can I do for you, Olivia?"

"Just calling to confirm our cave tour for Saturday. We've got one more than our original count, so that makes sixteen total."

"Okay, I'll make a note of that. Sixteen for Saturday at ten. Got it. See you then."

"Thanks. I'll see you."

I stop for a drink at the water fountain. As I bend down, my ears start to buzz. No, damn it, no!

Olivia!

I jerk my head, and the water shoots up and hits me in the eye. This time it sounded like Samantha was in the water fountain, calling my name. I back away, no longer thirsty.

I walk faster. If I can just stay focused on something else, maybe it will stop. I concentrate on my feet. Left. Right. Left. Right. Left.

Olivia!

Not listening. Left. Right. Left. Right. Left.

Olivia!

A little quieter, but still there. *Shut up already! You're not real.*
Left. Right. Left. Right. Left.

"Stop it!" I shout. It's lunchtime, and most of the students are already in the cafeteria, so no one hears me shout or sees me put my back against the row of lockers and slide to the ground. All of a sudden, I feel drained and exhausted. What's happening to me? I've gone from hearing Samantha's voice on the day of her funeral, which was freakin' bad enough, to hearing it multiple times a day?

This is so not normal.

I want to scream "Shut up!", but that's the fastest way to a padded room.

Deep breathing. That works for people, right?

I try it. Breathe in…breathe out…

It helps. Finally, I pull myself together and walk the rest of the way to the cafeteria. By the time I reach the door, Samantha's voice is only a whisper, and when it's my turn to pay, I realize I can't hear her anymore.

I take my tray over to where Julia is sitting with a bunch of our other friends. She's just finishing up her lunch. "That all you're eating?" she asks, pointing to my soup.

"I'm not that hungry."

"Where you been?" she asks.

"Talking to Mr. Cushing. You'll never believe what he asked me to do."

Her eyes get wide, and she raises her eyebrows.

"Oh, stop it. Not that." I punch her in the arm. "He asked me if I wanted to take Samantha's place on Student Council. Temporarily."

"Get out! You? Does that man have any grasp on reality?"

"Well you don't have to go that far," I say. "But it is somewhat of a stretch." I eat a spoonful of soup, but I still feel cold inside. "You would be perfect for the job. You're always helping out with school events. Why not put an official title on your efforts?"

"You know, you're right. Do you think Mr. Cushing is still in his room?"

"He doesn't seem like the brown bag type, but I don't see him here either, so probably."

"I'm off then!" She stands up and picks up her tray. "Oh, sorry. I don't mean to leave just as you get here."

"Don't worry about it. This will go down quickly. And then I'll grab a hot chocolate and catch up with everyone else."

"Uh, Olivia. It's September. They're not serving hot chocolate now."

"Right. I'll just eat my soup then. Go!"

Nineteen

OLIVIA

⊂◦⟩◦⊃

As I pull out the books I need to take home from my locker, I wonder if Jacob will be walking home from school. Probably not, since we jumped the battery in his truck when I dropped him off yesterday. I slam my locker door shut and allow myself to be swept down the hall by the crowd anxious to escape the building. As the throng surges through the open door, I hurry down the stairs, the warm September air chasing away the last bit of the chill I've felt most of the day. Since I'm watching my feet so I don't trip, I don't look up until I reach the last step. Jacob is on the grass off to the side as if he's waiting for someone. When our eyes link up, he comes closer and falls into step next to me.

"Mind if I walk you home?" he asks.

"Be my guest," I say, trying to keep from breaking out in too huge of a grin.

"I heard you like country music," he says.

"Really? Who told you that?"

"Nick. The guy in our chem class? He recruited me to play drums in his band. He mentioned you sometimes go to hear them play. I thought maybe you could hook me up with some current stuff. Tell me what's hot and what's not."

What's hot is the way the stubble drifts across his jawline. "Sure. I suppose so. You mind coming to my house? I'm supposed to put dinner in the oven."

"Yeah, sure."

We fall into a comfortable silence. Like he does every day, the dog on the corner barks like mad as we approach his yard. "Hold on a sec," Jacob says, sliding up next to the fence. He pulls something out of his pocket and slips it through the fence.

"Hey there, little guy. Here you go."

This is never going to work. That dog's going to bite his hand off. "You really shouldn't…"

But the little barker's tail starts wagging, and the barks turn into contented pants. His eyes close as Jacob scratches a spot on his back through the fence.

"Well, you little charmer," I say, half to myself.

Jacob gives one last scratch and then stands up and tosses another dog treat over the fence, which our new best friend captures expertly in his mouth and devours in two chews.

"Bye, Bud," Jacob calls over his shoulder as we continue down the street. "See you tomorrow."

"Is that your method for dealing with all of your enemies?" I ask.

"You mean bribery?" He pauses, pensive for a few moments. Then wrinkles appear on his forehead, and a frown overtakes his lips. "Nah. That's more my dad's thing."

Jacob's happy mood from before seems broken, and our silence doesn't seem as comfortable as we finish our walk to my house.

"This is it," I say, ambling up the sidewalk and the steps. The porch swing catches in the breeze and bumps against the wood on the front of the house.

"Wow. This is your house? It's huge. Three stories?"

"Yeah. A bit brutal to clean. But it's old. Early nineteen hundreds, Victorian. Meaning it didn't cost too much to buy. Just to heat, according to my mom."

"Was it in your family?"

"No. It was built by a woman architect. That was pretty rare for the time. My dad was an architect, and my mom teaches history at the college—her specialty is the Victorian era, so basically they both just fell in love with the house. I guess they planned on having lots of kids to fill it up. And on renting out the third floor as an apartment. Turns out they only had me. And after a few bad experiences with tenants before I was born, they stopped renting."

As I hold the door open for Jacob, I try to see the house through his eyes. The hardwood floors and oriental carpets in all the rooms and up the stairs. The Victorian era furniture and the piano I don't play anymore. The wallpaper covering generations of patterns beneath it.

"Yikes. That sounds ominous."

"I know. One guy kept a python up there, and it got out."

"Oh man. Did they ever find it?"

"My mom found it curled up in the washing machine. That's when she drew the line." I close the door behind us and motion toward the kitchen. "Let me pop in the lasagna. It'll just be a minute."

I slide the pan in the oven, then return to where I left Jacob and gesture toward the stairs. "Let's head up to the third floor," I say. "That is, if you want to see my favorite place in the whole house."

"With that type of introduction, how could I say no?"

We climb the stairs with only the steps making slight creaking noises in the quiet house. Wait. No voices inside my head. *Please let it stay that way.*

61

When we get to the third floor, it feels a bit hot and stuffy. "Let me open a window. You can put your stuff down anywhere."

"You do realize that you're living like a queen up here, right? Your own couch, refrigerator—is that a microwave?"

"Yeah, this is where I like to hang out. My bedroom is on the second floor. We don't heat this floor in the winter."

I go to the fridge, take out a container of raspberries, then rinse them and dump them in a bowl. I toss a couple in my mouth. Divine. "Sorry, you were probably hoping for something in the chip family. Let me put in some microwave popcorn. It's just that I have a weakness for raspberries."

"I'll keep that in mind," Jacob says. "What else is up here?"

I put in a bag of popcorn and hit Start on the microwave "Here, I'll show you." I point out the first room down the hall. "This was my dad's office."

"Was? Are your parents divorced too?"

"They got divorced when I was five, and then my dad died a few years after that."

"Oh, I'm sorry."

I never say stuff like "Don't be" or "It was a long time ago" because, really, it will never be long enough ago to stop that twinge of nausea every time I think of that day. So I simply say, "Thanks."

"Did your dad do that?" Jacob asks, pointing at a framed floor plan on the wall.

"Yeah, those were the plans for the dream house he was going to build us in Switzerland."

"I guess if you're going to dream, you might as well dream big. Why Switzerland?"

"It's where my parents met. At some crappy youth hostel. He wanted to go back in style, I guess. A house for the most beautiful woman in the world in the most beautiful country in the world."

"Wow. The guy was quite a romantic, wasn't he?"

"Yeah, I guess." Not the way I usually think about my dad, but hey.

The microwave dings. "I'll go grab the popcorn," I say. "Those doors over there lead out onto the balcony. We can hang out there if you want."

"Sounds perfect," Jacob says. "But you go sit. I'll get the snacks."

"Thanks." I open the doors to the balcony and bring out a couple of chairs and a small table.

Jacob returns with the popcorn and opens the bag, letting the steam escape. "Cool backyard. And a great view of the mountains in the distance."

"Yeah, I love it out here." I pull out my phone. "So. Let's find you some decent songs to listen to."

"Yes, please work your magic." Jacob tosses some popcorn in his mouth and hands me the bag. I grab a handful and continue scrolling through my playlists.

"Ooh, this is a good one," I say. "Thomas Rhett." I stand up and sway to the music, letting myself get lost in the beat. Jacob bobs his head back and forth, then stands up and dances alongside and with me, twirling me at all the right times.

"The percussion on this is awesome. We've got to have this in our set. What else you got?"

We listen to a dozen or more songs, sometimes dancing, sometimes just leaning against the railing and talking. Jacob's eyes light up when the percussion is particularly good, and he taps out the rhythm on the railing.

A slow song by Florida Georgia Line is up. I let the intro play. "I don't know about this one." I'm about to skip it when Jacob reaches over and brushes my hand away.

"Let it play," he says.

I shrug and set my phone on my chair. Jacob takes my right hand

63

in his left and puts his other on my back. His hands feel soft and comforting, the air smells of fall flowers, and Jacob's breath on my ear sends delightful shivers down my back. We sway and swirl, and my body melts into his, a sizzling current passing between us.

When the song is over, Jacob removes his hand from the small of my back and draws a circle with his thumb on the palm of the hand he's been holding. He looks down at me, and I know he's going to kiss me. My lips buzz in anticipation.

But then his brow furrows, and he almost seems to wince in pain. "I think I should go now," he says, his voice just barely more than a whisper. "I have my first band practice tonight, and I should eat something first. Something like dinner, I mean. The popcorn was great." He drops my hand completely now. "Thanks for playing the music. I think I get it now. Country, that is. At least a little bit."

What? Why didn't he kiss me? Doesn't he feel the same spark I do? "I'll walk you out," I say, trying not to show my disappointment.

We go downstairs, and Jacob says goodbye as if nothing has changed. But as I close the beveled glass door behind him, I watch him walk away, feeling like a bird in her cage with the door closed, alone.

Face it. He's just not that into you. He only asked you out to begin with because you were quote, "The only person I know."

Damn it!

Those damn green eyes. Those damn kissable lips.

Stop it! There's no future for us anyway. My voices show no signs of going away. Soon they will take over my life, like they did my dad's. And as much as I hate the voices, I'm also afraid of the medicine that might make them stop. And that is just stupid, stupid, stupid, because we all know what will happen if they don't stop.

In my room I think about what Jacob said, about my dad being a romantic. I stick my hand under my bed and pull out a plastic storage tub full of my dad's old architectural drawings. Taking out one of the long, rolled-up sheets, I slowly unfurl it. This is my favorite one, the one I should hate but instead love. Round and giant, the structure has tons of cool features, like a slide that goes from the second floor to the first and beds that roll out like drawers. The plans, to the uninformed eye, appear to be a futuristic space pod module. But I know better. This was my dad's true masterpiece. Plans for the interior of a marble. For the people who live inside.

What will Jacob think when he finds out that I'm crazy? What bits of normalcy will he remember about me? And will they be enough to bury all the ugly stuff?

Twenty

JACOB

᯽

*W*hile other states might have garage bands, I've just become a member of a carriage house band. Lots of the houses in town were built so long ago, people were driving horses and buggies. Nick's house is no exception. I guess people back then wanted to keep their distance from the smell of the horses. It works out well for Nick's parents since it also muffles the sound of our practice session. The outside of the building, a strange shade of green, is in serious need of a paint job, but the inside is surprisingly comfy, complete with old couches, little white lights wrapped around the rafters, and most important, an awesome looking drum set.

"Hey, y'all, here's the new drummer I was telling you about," says Nick.

Y'all? "You from the south, Nick?"

A tall skinny dude with a guitar strapped on puts Nick in a choke hold. "Naw. That's just Nick getting into the zone. I'm Zane, by the way." With his free hand he shakes my hand firmly. "And that over there is Katie." A cute blonde leaning against a bale of hay looks up and waves. "She's my sister, so don't get any ideas."

I chuckle. Good thing I have my eye on a certain waitress. "Nice to meet you all," I say, exaggerating the separation between the last two words.

Nick easily breaks out of Zane's grasp, grabs a cowboy hat off a stool, and smashes it down on Zane's head.

"You got a horse hiding here somewhere?" I say, gesturing at the hay.

"No. We used that in a photo shoot for our album cover."

"Album cover? Sounds serious."

"Not really. We've done a few weddings and such, nothing huge. But we've got a set at the school dance coming up, so we really need a drummer. And some practice. Ready to get down to it?"

"Sure thing," I say, pulling my sticks out of my pocket and making myself at home behind the drum set. As I play, I think about dancing with Olivia, the feel of her in my arms, the sweet smell of her hair. In her arms I felt transported to a different place, a different time, a different reality, one in which my brother wasn't dead and my parents still loved each other. The feeling was so overwhelming that even though I've only known her a few days, I feel like I've known her much longer. But just as I'd worked up the courage to kiss her, that weird déjà vu feeling was back. A sharp pain ripped through my heart, and I felt for a moment that if I kissed her, I would break my own heart. Just as quickly as the flash of whatever it was came, it was gone, but the spell was broken.

"So what do you think?" Nick asks after practice is over.

"Awesome," I answer truthfully. It feels great to be a part of a small band, just making music.

"Country's not driving you crazy?"

"Surprisingly not." It helps that it reminds me of Olivia.

"Don't worry. We don't just do country. In fact, maybe you can help us pick some more mainstream stuff for the dance. We'll be able to get away with a couple of country songs, but if that's all we do, the crowd will go crazy, and not in a good way."

"Sure, I can help you with that."

"All right then. Welcome to the band." We slap hands.

"Thanks. I'll see you tomorrow."

"See you."

I grab my sticks and head out into the night, taking a quick peek at the stars. At home in Michigan, my dad and I lived in the middle of nowhere, so I'm not used to all these streetlights interfering with my view.

"You into stargazing?" asks a voice behind me. Katie.

"Nothing serious. Just an admirer. You?"

"Same. You want to go grab a coffee?" she asks.

"Uh, what about your brother?"

"Zane? He's got his own plans."

"I'm talking about the part where he basically said you were off-limits."

"Zane's not my dad. I can make my own choices. So you in or not?"

"Thanks, but I'm kind of seeing someone else."

"Kind of?"

"It's not official but…"

"You'd like it to be?"

"A bit of a mind reader, aren't you?"

"It's not my only skill," she says. "Let me know if it doesn't work out."

Twenty-One

OLIVIA

The first yearbook meeting of the year is after school on Wednesday. It's also the first day I haven't walked home with Jacob. My lips curl into a smile as I think of him tossing the dog treat to that crazy barking dog yesterday.

"Earth to Olivia!"

"Huh?"

Julia is glaring at me. "I've asked you three times if you can come over next week to help me make decorations for the dance, but you've been lost in la-la land with that sappy grin on your face." Suddenly her eyes pop. "No! No way! Who is he, and why haven't you told me about him yet?"

"Since when does sappy grin have to mean 'guy'? Maybe I was thinking about...about...a cute dog I saw on my way home from school."

"Not buying it. The only dog on your way home from school is that psycho dog that won't stop barking."

"That dog's actually pretty nice."

"What'd you do? Slip it a tranquilizer?"

"No, just a treat."

"So after three years of continuous barking, you all of a sudden decide to start carrying dog treats?" She leans forward in her chair.

"Well, it wasn't actually me. It was Jacob. We were walking home together."

"Wait a minute. This isn't that hot new guy from Michigan, is it?"

"You know him?"

"I know *of* him, that's all. Unfortunately. Although from the look of that grin, I'd say he's off the market. I can't believe you didn't tell me! So you walked home together yesterday, is that it?"

"We actually walked home both Monday and Tuesday."

"My God! Was this your plan all along? You decided to start walking home so you could pick up hot guys? What a strategy! How come I didn't think of that? Do you think five miles is too far to walk?"

"Kind of. Though I suppose someone might offer to give you a ride."

"Brilliant!" She slaps her hand on the desk.

"Shh!"

"What? Don't you want the whole world to know who you're dating? Wait." She covers my hand with hers. "So have you been on an actual date? Where did you meet?"

"Well, we actually met at the diner—"

"Damn it!" She slaps the desk again. "I knew I should have gone for that job when you told me about the opening!"

"Julia, you already have a boyfriend, remember?"

"That's beside the point. So did you arrange to walk home from school right then?"

"No. I actually thought he was kind of a jerk."

"Oh no. No no no no no. Don't tell me you're dating a jerk. *This* is why you didn't tell me!" She shakes her head sadly.

"He's not actually a jerk. It's just when he saw my scar for the first time, he got kind of freaked out."

Julia starts making a clucking sound.

"But he apologized later. Said it was because he thought he recognized me from somewhere."

"Mmm." Julia looks unconvinced.

"Then we had chemistry class together, and he loaned me his jacket."

"Mmm!" Julia's tone brightens by several degrees. "Was that planned too?"

"Was what planned?"

"Asking to wear a jacket when it's been so hot out."

"No, I was actually cold. It was the day I was eating the soup."

"Right! Go on."

"So then we went to Laser Zap together."

"His idea or yours?"

"Mine."

"Okay, okay. This is sounding better. Now, let's get to the important question. Has there been lip-to-lip contact?"

My cheeks burn. "Uh, no."

"Okay, okay. The slow approach, nothing wrong with that. I can work with this."

"*You* can work with this? You know, Julia, this is why I didn't tell you until now. I don't need to be managed."

"Right. Of course not," she says, deflated.

"Julia, I…"

"Okay, everyone, let's get this meeting started," says Mrs. King, the yearbook advisor. "I wanted to start with a suggestion that I've heard from several people throughout the school. It's been proposed that we do a two-page tribute to Samantha in the yearbook, both with pictures and words. I've already gotten the approval of the principal, if this is something you want to move forward with. What does everyone think?"

"Sounds like a good idea," someone shouts from the back. There's a lot of positive murmuring and head nodding.

"Okay then. It looks like everyone is pretty much in agreement," says Mrs. King. "Now, who would like to take the lead on this?"

Once again I regret how I let our friendship fall apart. Maybe it was that guilt that led me to think I heard her voice. I look around the room. No one's hand is raised. I put mine in the air. "I'll do it."

Twenty-Two

JACOB

*O*n Friday, Olivia's waiting for me as I head out the front door of the school. I don't tell her it's my birthday. It doesn't even feel that special. "So you want to come over to my place?" I ask as we arrive at the barking dog's house.

"Yeah, sure," says Olivia, wrapping her wispy scarf back around her neck. It's one of those scarves that women wear to look pretty, not because it's cold out, because it isn't. And she does. Look pretty, that is.

"Here you go, Bruno!" I say, tossing him a dog treat.

"Bruno? How do you know his name?"

"I don't. He just looks like a Bruno, don't you think?"

Olivia looks skeptical. "Maybe?"

I reach over and take her hand, and she looks up at me with a little question in her eyes, as if she's wondering if this is real or if I'm going to have another freak-out like I did on the balcony above her backyard. I smile and squeeze her hand. Her eyes dance, and a smile pokes its way up one side of her face. She doesn't squeeze back, but she doesn't let go either, so I consider this a win. We walk like this, hand in hand, and even though my palm is a little sweaty, I almost don't want to get to my house because I don't want this feeling to end.

At home, I fish my key out of my pocket with my free hand and unlock the front door. Olivia follows me in. We're still holding hands. It's cooler indoors. Goodbye, calm. Hello, lust.

Olivia is gorgeous with that wisp of hair in her eyes. I'd like to unwrap that scarf and touch the skin on her neck. Kiss that delicate skin.

Keep it together, Jacob. Food. Think about food. Not Olivia.

Epic failure. I am hungry, but Olivia is still beautiful. So I let go of her hand and put all of my energy into being a gentleman.

Olivia inspects the walls. There are no family pictures. Just weird black-and-white photos, like the one with an escalator under water, and paintings, like the one with the melted clocks and the one with the guy in a top hat and an apple for a nose.

"So you live here with just your mom? She's not remarried?"

"No, she's still single." I open the fridge and pull out a couple of Cokes. I really have to talk to my mom about getting some more ginger ale here. "Although I think she's sleeping with someone."

"Oh." Olivia's cheeks turn a bit red.

"Sorry. I guess that was a little too much information." I hand Olivia a can and a glass.

"Just a bit abrupt is all. Cold, even."

"Yeah, I suppose you're right. I guess I should be happy for her." I open my own can and take a long drink. I don't bother with a glass.

"I guess," says Olivia. "Though I can kind of imagine how you feel."

"We can sit here at the counter." I plop myself down on a kitchen stool and gesture to another. This will be better than the couch. Less tempting.

"What makes you think she's sleeping with someone?"

"I found an extra coffee cup in the sink this morning."

"Maybe your mom forgot where she put her coffee. Had to pour a new cup."

"I also heard the front door open this morning, and right after that I saw some guy get into a car across from our house."

"Oh. Well, was he cute at least?"

"Cute?"

"Okay, was he handsome?"

"Don't you want to ask about his personality? Isn't that what you women find most important?"

"Of course. But you never said you actually talked to him."

"Oh. Right."

I hear a key in the lock, and the door swings open. Speak of the devil.

My mom looks surprised to see Olivia and I perched on the stools.

"You're home early," I say.

She sets a grocery bag on the counter. "I didn't know you were inviting anyone over to celebrate."

"Celebrate?" Olivia asks, her eyes widening.

"It's Jacob's birthday. He didn't tell you?"

Olivia smiles and shakes her head. "No. He didn't tell me. I'm Olivia, by the way." She sticks out her hand.

"Nice to meet you, Olivia," says my mom. "I hope you can join us for dinner."

"Oh, no, I was just stopping by on my way home," she says, jumping down from the stool.

"Don't go on my account. You have to at least stay for a piece of cake. There's no way we can eat the whole thing. I take that back—Jacob could probably eat the whole thing. Doesn't mean he should though. No need to wait until after dinner. We can dig in right now." With that, she whips out an Oreo cake from the grocery bag.

Olivia laughs. I like how it sounds.

"Oreo cake. Yum," Olivia says. "I guess I can be persuaded to help you out."

"Great. There's candles in the bag, Jacob," says my mom.

I pull a one and a seven from the bag, take off the cake lid, and stick them in.

"There's some matches in the drawer next to you, Olivia. You want to get the lights, Jacob? I'll get some paper plates from the pantry." My mom goes down the hall, and I stand by the lights, ready to turn them off once Olivia gets the candles lit.

Olivia takes the matches out of the drawer. She stares at them for a second, then drops them on the counter, shaking her head. "Sorry," she says. "Me and matches..."

Shit. Her arm. Of course that's how she got the scar.

"I got it," my mom says, setting the plates on the counter. As she lights the candles, I turn out the lights, and my mom starts belting out "Happy Birthday" in the worst singing voice imaginable.

When we finish the cake, Olivia gets up. "I should go," she says.

"Hold on. I'll walk you out."

On the porch, Olivia gives me a playful shove. "You should have told me it was your birthday!"

"It's no big deal. It's not like I'm five or something."

"Still. I would have given you something." She raises her eyebrows.

"Really now? Well, maybe I could give you something instead."

"And what would that be?"

I'm about to kiss her when my mom opens the front door. Really, Mom? She must notice us spring apart because she says, "Sorry, don't mind me. I'm just going for the mail."

As my mom heads for the mailbox, Olivia clears her throat. "I guess you can save that for some other time." Her cheeks pink up and she gives a quick wave as she walks down the sidewalk.

When my mom comes back from the mailbox she asks, "Should we get a pizza?"

I shrug. "Pepperoni and green olives?"

She grimaces. She's always hated green olives. "I'll take mushrooms on my half."

My mom calls for the pizza, and I go hang out in my room. I make my way through the country playlist on my phone, tapping out the rhythms on my drum set.

Fifteen minutes later, my mom's looming in my doorway. "Can you go pick up the pizza?"

I nod, setting my drumsticks on the dresser, then follow her to the kitchen and grab my keys from the counter. As I head out to the truck, she shoves a card into my hands. "This is from your dad."

"I don't…"

"Just take it, Jacob. And here's money for the pizza."

I sigh and take them both. In the truck, I hold the envelope in my hands, inspecting it. The handwriting's not my dad's. I guess he couldn't be bothered to address it himself. Sophia must have done it. I don't want to deal with this shit between my dad and me right now, so I pop open the glove box and shove the card in, mangling it in the process.

I run my fingers over the marks on the dash on the passenger side. Remnants of me riding shotgun with my dad, sticks in hand, using the dashboard as a drum set. That had to have been annoying as hell, but he never said anything—except when I tried to turn the rearview mirror into a cymbal.

I shake my head, doing my best to dislodge the memories, and turn the key.

When I get back, my mom and I eat in silence except for the part where she asks me about my day and I grunt. Not because I'm trying to be a jerk, but because I don't really like talking about my day. I'm mean, it's school.

As I shove the last bite of pizza in my mouth and stand up, my mom says, "Hold on there. You have to open your present."

"I already told you I don't want the car."

"Yes, Jacob. I know." She's pissed off. "I mean the present from me. It's in my car."

"Oh. Okay. Thanks."

We troop out to the garage together, and she opens the trunk. The box is so big she had to put down all the seats, including the one for the front passenger. It's one of those portable basketball hoops you can set up on the driveway.

"The man at the store said you put water or sand in the bottom part after you get it where you want it. I thought it would be easier to get this kind than the one you have to put in with concrete."

"Right. Definitely easier." Also less permanent.

"Your dad said you liked playing ball at his house."

"Yeah, I did. Thanks, Mom."

She looks down at the box uncertainly, hands on her hips. "I can help you put it together if you want."

"Nah, I got it."

"You sure?"

I nod and bite my lip and try not to think about the one thing my dad left out of what he told her.

The part where he and I used to play together.

After my mom goes back inside, I grab some tools from the garage and get to work on the net. While I'm busy lining up all the screws, my phone vibrates. It's a text from my dad.

Happy birthday from both of us.

Pretty smart move on his part, texting instead of calling. Makes it impossible for me to hang up on him.

Twenty-Three

JACOB

As I pull up in front of Olivia's house Saturday morning, she's waiting for me on the porch swing, her hair up and securely fastened in preparation for our excursion to the cave. It's my first official event as a member of the Outdoor Adventure Club.

"Thanks for the ride," Olivia says, climbing into my truck and slamming the door. She pushes a free strand of hair behind her ear.

"No problem."

"So what did you get for your birthday?" She settles in and puts on her seatbelt.

"My mom got me a basketball hoop for the driveway."

"That's cool. You play a lot back home?"

"All the time with my dad. Until recently, that is."

She glances over, a curious look in her eye. "Did he get you something?"

I pull out onto the street. "He tried to give me a car, but I told him I didn't want it. Or rather I told my mom to tell him that."

"Come again?"

"Yeah, I know. Pretty dumb move. It was a Mustang. Red."

"What? I'm guessing you have your reasons?"

"He was just trying to make up for sending me here. I wasn't ready to let him feel better about it."

"Oh. Don't you want to be here?"

"I don't know. When my parents divorced, I said I wanted to live with my dad, and my mom didn't seem to care. So…"

"Now you think that neither one of them wants you around?"

"Maybe?"

"What's that expression—if you love something, let it go? Maybe she was just giving you space? Hoping you'd come back?"

"What, like a bird?"

"I'm kind of anti-bird at the moment, so let's just say like the little boy she raised?"

As we reach the city limits, I shift into fifth and let her rip. "Anti-bird? How exactly do you become anti-bird?"

"It's just, they seem to be in my way all the time lately. Diving in front of me, banging into my windshield, pooping on me, singing too loudly."

I laugh. "Singing too loudly? What, do you live in a forest preserve? How are they singing too loudly?"

"I guess that does sound a bit harsh." She smiles.

"And pooping on you? I have never, in all my seventeen years, been pooped on by a bird." I'm laughing so hard I have to wipe a tear out of the corner of my eye.

"Okay. I made that part up. But at the moment, I really don't like birds."

"Duly noted. So what do you like? Besides me, that is." I look over at Olivia. She's rolling her eyes.

"Kidding," I say.

"Right. So what do I like? I like climbing and basically anything outdoors..."

"Except birds."

"Right. Except birds."

Twenty-Four

OLIVIA

We strap on our climbing gear and helmets and turn on our lights as Mr. Cushing thanks our host for giving us a tour of his cave. Like the other caves on private property in the area, this one is not open to tourists, but is by invitation only.

"I'm Jeff Wilson, president of the Ridgewood Grotto Club," begins our host, "and with me is fellow Ridgewood Grotto Club member Kevin Shipman. Between the two of us, we should be able to answer any questions you have about the cave and help you navigate the narrow tunnels as well as rappel to the lower level. Before we get started, is anyone afraid of the dark or enclosed spaces?"

There are a few nervous titters, but no one speaks up.

"Okay then. Let's go spelunking!" says Jeff.

With only our headlamps to illuminate the way, we follow Jeff, our feet crunching on the rocky cave floor. A stream of water falls from above and soaks a corner of my right shoulder. Jeff stops in front of what looks like a giant wormhole. "This will be our passageway to the next chamber," he says. "The passage does get slightly narrower before we're through, but not much. You should all fit through with no problem."

"We *should* fit through? He expects us to crawl through that?" Jacob mutters, his warm breath next to my ear. "I suppose it doesn't bother you though, since you like climbing."

"I like climbing, but I'm not as much of a fan of crawling into holes when I can't see through to the other side."

"You suppose there'll be bugs in there, or don't bugs live in caves?"

"Are you nervous or something?"

"Me? Nervous? Afraid of a few creepy crawlies?" He guffaws. "You bet your ass I am. Now get in there before I go running out of here like a chickenshit."

I laugh.

"Sorry, was that too much swearing? I tend to swear when I'm scared shitless. Oops. There I go again."

A little bit of my own nervousness fades away, and as the shoes of the person ahead of me fade from view, I hoist myself into the tunnel.

I pull myself forward, focused on getting to the end. A chill settles through the tunnel, and I'm kicking myself for not bringing a warmer sweatshirt. It's quiet except for some undecipherable shouts from ahead and a buzzing sound. Damn it. That buzzing sound always means...

One, two, three.

It's a little boy's voice, one I don't recognize. Even though I don't like it, I prefer it over hearing Samantha.

Four, five, six.

The words seem to be swirling all around me, echoing off the walls of the narrow tunnel.

Seven, eight, nine, ten!

My heart starts thumping harder than it should, and my stomach feels like it's been weighed down by a buoy. I don't like this. I don't like this at all. I freeze, feeling myself shutting down. I need the voices to stop. Not just now, but forever.

"Hey!" My foot is being wiggled up and down. "You're killing me here, Olivia. Keep moving before I run out of sweat!" Jacob's words snap me out of my stupor. I crawl forward relentlessly, barely able to concentrate over the imaginary chatter.

Yes! Finally the end! I surge forward with one more burst of energy. As I slide out the end, hands grab my arms and help me regain my footing. Seconds later, Jacob's head appears, and I help him out of the tunnel. "Geez, Olivia. Way to freak a guy out with that mid-tunnel vacation you took."

I smile weakly and try to push the little boy's voice to the back of my mind. Jacob runs a hand through his hair. There's a smudge on his cheek. "Just trying to keep you on your toes, Jacob."

One-two-three-four-five-six.

"On my toes? How did you expect me to be on my toes when I was slithering on my stomach?"

One-two-three-four-five-six.
One-two-three-four-five-six.
One-two-three-four-five-six.

"Shh!" I say, more to the little boy's voice, which has gotten louder, than to Jacob. "You better listen to the rappelling instructions."

"Oh, I've got the most important part down pat. The part that says I'm going before you. I'm not hanging halfway between here and a bottomless pit while you stop to admire the scenery."

I concentrate on Jeff and Kevin, act like I'm at a concert or something, where there are thousands of voices around you, but you don't really notice. White noise, they call it. Noise you don't focus on.

I focus on Jeff and Kevin. Only them. Jeff and Kevin.

They demonstrate how to prepare our ropes and clip in and have everyone practice by grabbing the rope and belaying themselves a few feet here on firm ground. The little boy's voice has quieted to a whisper, and I'm feeling more like myself.

True to his word, Jacob inserts himself into the rappelling line in front of me, giving me a self-satisfied nod as he clips on and heads down. When we get the all clear that Jacob has reached the bottom, I clip in, and Kevin checks to make sure I'm good to go. But the second he does, the voice in my head grows louder once again, drowning out any last-minute instructions. *One-two-three-four-five-six.* What's with all the counting? I let myself down as fast as possible, rappelling down the shaft almost at a free fall, slowing myself only when I can tell I'm near the end.

When my feet touch ground, I unclip and get as far away from the shaft as possible. "Holy hell," says Jacob. "Sure, I complained about how slow you were in the tunnel, but you didn't have to take it as a challenge to skyrocket down the next part. You're one crazy girl, aren't you?"

If you only knew. "Let's get out of here," I say.

I find Mr. Cushing and ask, "Is it okay if we head out, or do we have to wait for the group?"

"Go ahead. The exit's straight out that way," he says, pointing.

"Thanks," adds Jacob. "That was certainly exhilarating!"

"Glad you enjoyed it," says Mr. Cushing.

The voice is relentless. *Seven-eight-nine-ten.* I take off, head down, focused on the ground, going as fast as possible. Jacob struggles to keep up with me and manages to do so only when I stumble and have to stop to steady myself. *One-two-three-four-five-six-seven-eight-nine-ten.*

"I would say you should stop and smell the roses, but in this case I guess we're not going to find any roses until we get outside. Still, could you maybe slow down just a little bit?"

"I just want to get out of here," I say. "I'm cold, wet, dirty, and a little miserable."

"And here I thought I was the only one." He takes a giant step from one rock to another, avoiding a big puddle, then holds out his hand to me. I grab it and join him on the teetering rock before he abandons it for the next, helping me navigate that one as well. We stick to the right for a bit, avoiding the foot-soaking puddles to the center, until the water disappears and we're able to walk side by side again, still holding hands. A bit of sunlight peeks out from ahead, and minutes later we're back outside.

"Ah, glorious civilization," Jacob says, collapsing against a boulder outside the cave and pulling me in next to him. "Can I still get my dues back for the Outdoor Adventure Club?" he asks.

"Dues? There aren't any dues."

"Darn it. I thought if I faked poverty, you might not notice that the outdoors and I aren't as friendly as I'd like us to be."

"Don't worry. After today, I'm not sure of my own membership status."

My shoulders relax as I realize that the little boy's voice has faded to a whisper. "Of course, we're going paintballing next month…"

"Ooh, game on," Jacob says.

Let's just hope I'm not checked into a mental ward by then.

Twenty-Five

OLIVIA

It's Labor Day, and my mom invites me to her faculty picnic. This is an event to be avoided at all costs—unless you like listening to infomercials about Ancient Greece or the mating rituals of African tortoises. So I tell her I have something really important to do for school. Which I do. Then I slip out of the house and drive to Samantha's.

As I wait for someone to answer the door, I realize that it's been almost forty-eight hours since I stumbled out of that cave, forty-eight hours since I last heard any voice that didn't belong. Maybe I should just leave now. I'm sure someone else would be happy to step up.

But just as I turn to head back down the steps, the door opens. "Hi, Olivia. Come on in," says Mrs. Young.

Suck it up, Olivia. You can do this.

"Thanks for letting me stop by. Like I said on the phone, we just wanted a few pictures for a yearbook tribute on Samantha. But it's not a rush. I could come back in a couple of weeks, or even next month if that would be better."

"No, no, now is fine," she says, gesturing for me to follow her. We pass through the kitchen and then the den, where Cara is playing with marbles again. I hold my breath. But there are no voices. And I don't believe there are people in marbles. That has to count for something.

Mrs. Young shows me to Samantha's room. "I'll leave you here," she says, her voice pinched. "Just come find me if you need anything."

"Thank you. I will."

I get out my phone and slowly scan the room. Samantha's purple-and-gold pom-poms hang by their wrist straps from the knobs on the closet door. She was the flyer for the cheerleading squad at football games. I flash back to the last game I saw her cheer at, leading the crowd from her perch high above. I quickly snap a photo. On her nightstand is a copy of a Sarah Dessen novel, and I remember that Samantha always did like to read. I frame the book in the shot, slightly off-center, a tattered bookmark peeking out over the edge of the pages, marking a spot Samantha would never return to. I'm not the world's greatest photographer, but this feels more like finding a story than taking pictures. A bunch of ribbons with medals are draped over the top corners of the dresser mirror. I take another photo, then reach up and pull one down so I can read it. It's from track. The mile. As I run my fingers over the grooved letters and the image of a shoe with a pair of wings, my ears start to buzz, and the edges of the medal suddenly seem fuzzy and out of focus. I startle when Samantha's voice erupts from one of the wings, as loud as if it's coming from a megaphone—*Run!*

I probably should've been expecting it, but I wasn't. I fumble the medal, which smacks against the top of the dresser, then plummets to the floor to bury itself in the fibers of a small purple shag rug.

My right hand trembles slightly, and my stomach feels as if I've just gotten off a roller coaster. I have to get out of here. I bolt from the room, slowing only when I reach the kitchen. The burgundy paint on the walls makes me think of blood. Near the ceiling there's a wallpaper border with the faces of smiling cows—only today they seem to be laughing, laughing at me. I try not to look at them directly, but catching glimpses of them out of the corner of my eye only makes them seem more judgmental. Mrs. Young is at the table with a box of pictures in front of her. She's absorbed by one of Samantha crossing the finish line at a Save the Manatee race.

Noticing me, she places the photo back in the box and carefully secures the lid. "Here," she says. "You can borrow these. Just bring them back when you're done."

I scoop up the box and try not to appear too anxious to leave. "Thanks, Mrs. Young. I'll get them back to you right away."

She nods. "I was wondering, Olivia, if you might be able to babysit for Cara and Owen tomorrow? He was the little boy who was here playing with Cara..." She trails off, but I know she means on the day of the funeral. "I promised his mom I would go with her to a book club meeting, and my husband has a work thing. I couldn't care less about the book club, but my neighbor, she means well. I know she's just trying to get me out of the house, and I know she's right because when I'm here, all I do is cry, and then Cara wants to know why and, well, it's not good for Cara either. I mean, she needs me too. Or maybe I'm the one who needs her now more than ever."

I can tell Mrs. Young isn't really talking to me; she's really just trying to convince herself, and I'm okay with that. All I want to do is get out of here and away from Samantha's room and that medal and the mantel in the next room where there's no longer a bird staring down at us because I broke it, all because Samantha picked her own funeral to shout at me. I mean, that's when my delusion took over, and it's probably not good for me to be here surrounded by all these things that used to belong to Samantha because they are obviously one of my triggers, but what can I say to Mrs. Young? I can't very well tell her that I heard her dead daughter talking to me from a bird figurine and now a medal and that the cows on the wallpaper might be laughing and that's why I really need to stay away from this house. So instead I say, "No problem, Mrs. Young. What time should I be here?"

"Is six-thirty okay?"

"Six-thirty is just fine," I say.

Twenty-Six

OLIVIA

"Remind me why we're making tissue paper flowers for a dance that's not going to happen?" I say to Julia as I fight with a particularly difficult piece.

"It's not going to be canceled," says Julia. "The Sweet Dreams Strangler has never killed two girls in the same city. But just to be on the safe side, the administration is going to have parent volunteers to monitor the parking lot and escort people to and from the doors."

"Your idea?"

"Yes, actually."

"Not bad, Miss Student Council President."

Julia chucks a paper bird at me. "Member-at-large, thank you. Maybe next year I'll try for president." She picks up the mangled flower I've just finished out of the stack. "I'm thinking maybe you should stick to making birds."

Birds are the last thing I want to be making, but I pick up a giant piece of square paper anyway. Fold in half, unfold, fold in half again.

As I make the first diagonal fold, I think about the words coming out of the beak of the bird figurine on Samantha's mantel. *Stop him.* Five victims. Five cities. Stop the killer? How could I stop the guy who is doing this? In all likelihood, the guy isn't even from around here, isn't even from this state. He started in Ohio, for God's sake, making his way east along the expressway. Until his latest victim, the girl in Essex. Why did he go backward? And was he going to continue that way or swing back around this way?

I push the creases down on the paper, making a kite shape. Either way, what can I do about it? It's not like I could possibly know the guy personally, right? He killed teenage girls, but what were the chances that he knew any of his victims? Still, the voices at school bothered me. Could this guy be a teacher, someone teenage girls would trust? Someone like Mr. Cushing?

I smack down my newly formed bird wings a bit forcefully. Damn it, Olivia! The voices aren't messages from real dead people; they're proof of just how crazy you're becoming. Proof of how you should see a doctor. Pronto.

My phone pings. A text from Jacob. My heart beats a little quicker.

I'll see a doctor soon. Just not yet. Because as soon as I have proof of my crazy, this thing with Jacob, it will be all over. I know it will.

What you doing?

"Who's that?" asks Julia.

"Just Jacob," I say, trying to sound nonchalant.

"Whoa, back the truck up here. The last time I saw you get that much scarlet on your face while saying a guy's name, it led to a six-month hot and heavy relationship."

"Do you have to use the term 'hot and heavy'? It sounds so juvenile."

"Fine. I'll stop using the term. But notice you haven't exactly denied an intense attraction."

"Do you mind? I'm trying to type."

Helping Julia make paper birds for the dance.

"How come I haven't met him yet?" Julia whines.

Jacob's reply comes back.

Need help?

I keep my phone close so Julia doesn't see what I'm typing.

Folding or getting out of here?

"Well?" says Julia. I glance back at my phone.

Either one. Send address.

"He's on his way," I say.

Twenty-Seven

JACOB

I find directions to Julia's house on my phone, then I leave a note for my mom, just in case she comes back before I do. Yeah, right.

I step out into the cool night air, then climb in my truck and start it up. The rumbly engine makes me smile. Truth is, I didn't really say no to a new car because I wanted to say "screw you" to my dad. Somehow this truck represents me and my dad and all of the good times we had together. Before the truck was mine, it was his.

I remember lying in the truck bed looking up at fireworks, my dad right next to me. Dad driving us to the beach at Lake Michigan, where we swam all afternoon and then piled back in it, the sand between our toes. Going all the way to the Detroit suburbs for a Pistons basketball game in it. Will my dad be able to figure this out even though I didn't have the words to tell him? Probably not.

When I get to Julia's house, her mom lets me in and takes me to where the girls are working. A girl who must be Julia is focused on a flower made of red tissue paper. Olivia is staring strangely at a paper

94

bird. When she sees me, a smile spreads slowly across her face, and she sends the bird sailing toward me. I snatch it out of the air.

"What's up?" I say. I send the bird back to Olivia, who ducks instead of catching it.

"Hey there," she says. "Meet Julia."

Julia looks up. "So nice to finally meet you," she says. "Olivia's told me a lot about you."

"Really?" I say.

"Not so much," Julia admits. "Just enough that I know she likes you."

"Julia!" Olivia says, snatching the flower out of her hand.

"So I take it you've got a tropical theme going on?" I ask.

"Yes, it's for the *dance* at school," Julia says. She looks pointedly at me and then back at Olivia.

"Jacob knows about the dance," Olivia says. "He's playing drums for Nick's band."

"Oh, great. But you guys aren't playing the whole time, right? So you'll have some time to dance too?"

I laugh. "Yes, we'll have some free time too."

"You guys want some chips?" Julia asks suddenly.

"Sure," Olivia and I answer, almost in unison.

Julia leaves the room, and I sit on the floor next to Olivia.

"Sorry about Julia's pretty blatant matchmaking. She sees it as her calling."

"Don't worry about it," I say. "So, you going to the dance?" I try to sound nonchalant, but it doesn't come out that way.

"I don't know. My mom probably won't go for it even with the escorts Julia's lining up for the parking lot."

I clear my throat. "So you don't have a date then?" *Wow, Jacob. Could you sound any more uncool?*

"Nope," says Olivia. She picks up one of the birds and blasts it at the ceiling. It spirals back down and lands at my feet.

"Say you had a date. Would your mom let you go then?"

"Are you asking me out? Because if it's just to get your hands on my Jeep, the answer's no."

"Actually it's to get my hands on you," I say. I worry for a moment that I've said the wrong thing, but then she laughs.

"Really now?" she taunts.

"Maybe," I say, and I toss a paper bird back at her. It gets stuck in her hair.

We hear Julia coming down the hall, singing at the top of her lungs.

"In that case, it's a date."

Twenty-Eight

OLIVIA

"*O*oh, yum." My mom grabs a fork from the drawer and spears a pineapple chunk from the carton in front of me. "I was just about to watch a—"

Don't say documentary. Don't say documentary.

"A documentary about…"

I tune out the rest of the sentence. I hate documentaries.

"You want to join me?" My mom spears another pineapple.

"Huh?"

"I said, do you want to watch a—"

"Sorry. No can do. I have to go to the bookstore. It's for a school project."

Her eyes light up. "What's the topic?"

"I haven't quite decided yet. It's for science." That's not completely a lie. The book I need is scientific. It's just not for school.

"Oh. Can't help you with that." She stabs another pineapple. "You need some money?"

"No, it's fine. Thanks anyway." I grab one more pineapple for myself, then drop my fork in the sink. "Enjoy your show." *I'm sure you'll tell me all about it when I get home.*

She breaks out in a big grin. "I'll tell you about it at dinner."

I give a wave and head out to the Jeep. I'm actually going to buy a book on schizophrenia. I mean, the Internet is helpful and all, but it's just that. The Internet. A place where there's a lot of right but also a lot of wrong. And there are some things you just need to make sure you get right.

I once asked my mom how she knew my dad was sick. She said my dad started complaining that he was having trouble at work. That everyone was against him and that the boss treated him unfairly. Finally it got so bad that my mom went to talk to my dad's boss herself and asked him what he had against my dad. The boss looked at her real funny and said her husband wasn't actually working. He was just sitting at his desk not doing anything at all, and they were going to have to let him go.

Next to the bookstore is an empty lot, overgrown with long grasses and some trees. Today there are also birds. Hundreds of them. Flitting, flying, swooping around. Squawking and making noise. They all seem to be the same kind. Some type of brown bird. Small, ugly, somewhat boring. Have they already started their migration now, in September?

It takes me a while to find the right section in the bookstore, but once I'm there, picking the book itself is pretty easy. I just grab one with a comforting title and a soothing cover with no traces of birds or marbles.

Back at home, my mom has dinner ready on the table. Parmesan chicken with a side of…ancient Mesopotamia, from the look of the notes next to her plate. "You missed a good one," she says. "Find what you needed?"

"Yep. I'm just going to go put it away." I take the stairs two at a time to the third floor, to my dad's office, where my mom never ever goes. Then I unzip the cushion on the burgundy armchair and slide the book in. A lot of the stuffing is missing, so there's plenty of room for it and the notebook that's already there. *Just get rid of that thing already, Olivia.* My fingers grasp the spiral binding, and I bring it as far as the zipper. And then I hesitate. This notebook is not the kind of thing you just throw out. It's the kind of thing you burn. And that is something I most definitely cannot do.

After dinner I take a long bath in the claw-foot tub in my bathroom, a place that, despite new paint and a puppy dog print, always looks like it belongs in a different century. I think about birds and voices and Jacob. Well, I think mostly about Jacob. And the longer I soak, the less I want to read that book in the burgundy cushion.

I will read it. I really will.

Just not tonight.

Twenty-Nine

OLIVIA

*S*trangely enough, when I babysat for Cara and Owen, I didn't hear any voices, and the kids managed to not play with marbles, so all in all it was a good experience. Samantha's mom and her friend were happy with how well I did, so now here I am at Owen's house babysitting just him. I don't do a lot of babysitting, but I have to say that Owen is pretty fun. It's a good thing he hasn't asked me to read one of the Babar books on his shelf, though, because that's just not happening. I love elephants, but I hate Babar. Babar is an elephant that wears a green suit and has some sort of adventures, I think. I don't really know because I had one book about Babar, but when I gave it to my dad to read to me, he got stuck on the part where Babar steps into an elevator. Dad just kept reading it over and over again. And laughing. It wasn't funny. He was just laughing. And I was begging him to turn the page. But he wouldn't. He just kept reading that same sentence over and over. Finally my mom came into the room and announced that our visit was over and my dad needed to go back to his apartment.

The next day I ripped out all the pages and tried to flush them down the toilet. I wasn't quite successful and my mom was pretty pissed, but at least she threw the book out and announced she wouldn't be getting me another copy. She never did ask why I did it. How many bad things do kids do, not because they're trying to be bad, but because they're trying to fix the way they feel inside?

Ready or not!

I look over at Owen. He's busy building a three-legged dog out of Legos.

"What was that?"

"It's a tree! Can't you tell?"

"Well, of course. I mean, what did you say?"

"I didn't say anything."

Ready or not!

"Is that one of your friends?"

"Is who one of my friends? The tree? No, trees can't be friends, silly! But sometimes they're mean, like in *The Wizard of Oz*."

I stand up. "I need to go check on something outside. Can you stay here and keep playing with the Legos?"

"Yep," he says without looking up.

Ready or not!

The voice is definitely coming from the backyard. It's a little boy's voice. It sounds so happy.

I open the sliding glass door and go out into the backyard. I stand there and wait, like when a smoke detector is low on batteries, but you can't tell which one it is, so you have to stand there and wait until it chirps again. Their backyard is a child's paradise, with a play set and a tree house. The closest neighbors are so far away you can't even see their houses, and the property backs up to woods.

Ready or not!

The toy bin. It's definitely coming from the toy bin. I open the lid, bracing myself for spiders and other insects, but none jump out at me. I take the toys out and line them up on the ground. A fake lawnmower, a croquet set, a Frisbee, some chalk, a plastic bat and glove, a jump rope.

I wait.

Ready or not!

The bat. It's definitely the bat. I put all the other toys back in the bin and close the lid, then I move away from the house, the bat in my hands. Slowly I hold it up against my ear.

Ready or not!

Damn it!

Yep, definitely from the bat. I shake the thing, trying to see if there is some sort of voice recorder in it.

Ready or not!

There has to be something inside of this. If I could just open the bat up and get it out. It is plastic, after all.

I smack it against the tree. Again. And again. Then I grab one of the stakes from the croquet set and a mallet, and I place the stake against the bat and swing the mallet. I swing over and over again, and at first the bat just flattens, but then finally I punch a hole in it. I shake it, looking for the electronic piece that will tell me I'm not crazy.

Of course I don't find it.

As I stare at the flattened bat, I wonder if there will come a time that I won't even remember when voices didn't control my life. Maybe I'll disappear into some world where I'm laughing all the time at some private joke between me and those people living in marbles.

"What ya doin'?" I whip around. It's Owen.

"Oh, nothing. I mean, there was this really big bug, so I killed it with the bat." My heart pounds so wildly, it's hard to get the words out.

"Cool! Can I see?"

"There's not really anything left to see. Sorry, bud. And I kind of broke your bat. But I promise I'll get you a new one. I'm just going to put this one in my car so I know what kind of bat to get you. Can you go back inside while I do that?"

My voice shakes, but Owen seems not to notice. Instead he nods and skips off to the house. I force myself to take deep breaths as I walk to the car and pop the trunk open just wide enough to toss in the bat. Then I collapse on the curb and clutch my hair with my hands, trying desperately to pull out the crazy.

Thirty

JACOB

*text Olivia.

What you up to?

Babysitting. Want to come help?

Uh...Is that even allowed?

Don't know, but I don't feel so well. Either you're up or I give in and call the parents.

Text me the address.

She does, and fifteen minutes later I'm knocking on the sliding glass door in the back, as instructed.

Olivia opens the door and lets me in the kitchen. The kid is at the table, chowing down on a hot dog.

"Maybe this isn't such a good idea," she whispers. "I'm feeling a little better, and on second thought, I don't know what the parents would think about you being here. I feel bad about making you come all the way here. I tried to text you, but you didn't answer."

"Maybe because I was driving? That whole texting and driving thing?"

"Oh, right. That. Good for you."

"Who's that?" asks the little kid.

Olivia turns around. "Owen, meet my friend Jacob," she says. "He was just saying hi."

"Hi, Jacob," Owen says, a blob of ketchup bursting out of the side of his mouth. "Wanna hot dog?" he asks, picking one up from a platter and holding it in the air.

I shrug. "Sure. I won't turn down food."

Owen gets up, still gripping my hot dog, opens a cupboard at ground level, pulls out a plastic plate, and plops the wiener on it. Then he sets the plate on the table and pats the seat next to him. "You can sit here," he says.

"Actually, I was going to take mine to go."

Owen's face turns all red, and I think he might actually cry.

"You know, on second thought, I think I will stay." I cross to the refrigerator, and my arm brushes Olivia's, maybe on purpose. It leaves my arm feeling like I stuck a fork in a toaster, but in a good way. I open the refrigerator. "Got any mustard in here, Owen?"

"Daddy likes mustard," Owen says.

"Got it." I grab the mustard and sit down next to Owen. Olivia hands me a napkin. Then she sits down with us and stabs a piece of pineapple with her fork.

"Aren't you having a dog?" I ask.

"Not now that you're eating mine," she answers.

My eyes go wide. "Oops. Here, have some."

"Just kidding," she says, popping the piece of pineapple into her mouth. "There's a whole extra package in the fridge. I just wanted to see your eyes pop out like that."

Owen bursts out in a belly laugh. "Do it again, Jacob!"

I try for the same effect with my eyes. Owen roars with laughter once again.

When we finish our hot dogs, Owen announces, "Let's play Candy Land."

"Sure," says Olivia. "Do you know where it is?"

"Jacob get it," he says, taking hold of my hand and getting up.

"Okay, you boys get the game, and I'll clear the table," Olivia says.

Owen leads me into the living room and points to a bookshelf. "Up there," he says. I grab the game, and Owen scoops a stuffed alligator from the floor.

"We can set up in here," Olivia calls from the kitchen. "I just wiped the table."

I open the box on the table and take out the pieces while Olivia slides all the cards into a big misshapen pile and tries to shuffle them. Owen sets the alligator on an empty seat. "Allie's going to play too," he says. "My old babysitter Samantha gave me Allie. She's nice, but she's dead now." He grabs a game piece from the table. "I always get to be the red guy, and Allie is the green guy." He tilts his head at me. "You can be the blue guy," he says, handing it to me. "And you can be the yellow one," he says to Olivia. He holds the piece out to her. She takes it, but Owen doesn't let go. "Are you going to die?"

Olivia looks away for a second, then forces a smile and says, "No, Owen. Of course not." She rubs his back, and Owen opens his hand and gives her the yellow piece. He then explains the rules for us, emphasizing how the youngest person goes first. "That's Allie," he clarifies. "Then me."

The game progresses well. I'm actually winning until a gumdrop card sends me back to almost the beginning. This elicits another belly laugh from Owen.

"Allie's tired of sitting by herself," Owen says. "Can she sit on your lap, Olivia?"

"Hmm. Let me think about that. Will she behave?"

"Let me ask her," Owen says. "Allie, can you be a good little alligator and sit on Olivia's lap?"

"She says, 'Okay,'" Owen announces, handing the stuffed animal to Olivia, who holds it against her chest with one arm.

Owen wins the first game and does a little happy dance. "You want to play again?" he asks eagerly.

"Of course. You have to give me a chance to beat you," I say, scooping up the cards and reshuffling them.

"Allie is first again," Owen insists. "Do you want to go for Allie, or do you want me to?" he asks Olivia, who has her eyes closed.

"Why don't you go for Allie," I say. Olivia is starting to shiver. "You know, Olivia gets cold a lot. Do you have a blanket she can use?"

"Yes," says Owen, popping up and running off.

I get up and stand behind Olivia, putting my arms around her.

Owen comes back with a Spider-Man blanket. "Here, let's put it around her shoulders," I say. We wrap the blanket around her.

"Why don't you take your turn, Owen?" I say.

"Allie first, then me!" he says.

"Right."

Owen takes the turns, and then I go. "What, I only get to go one spot?" I complain.

Owen squeals with delight. "Your turn, Olivia!" he shouts.

Olivia's eyes are still closed. "You know, I don't think she's feeling too well. How about I go for her too?" I say.

"Is she going to die?" he asks, looking concerned.

"No, no—she just missed her nap today." I take a card and move for Olivia.

"I missed my nap yesterday, and I didn't fall asleep early," Owen says proudly.

"Oh. Well, that's good. Look, Owen, Allie got the ice cream cone!" I say, switching out the cards to distract him.

"Yay!" Owen shouts, moving the piece.

"I'm just going to help Olivia over to the couch so she can finish her nap," I say.

"I'm fine," Olivia says, but she gets up and leans against me. We shuffle over to the couch in the living room. "Let me just lie down for a minute. Are you sure you can handle…"

"I'm rocking Candy Land," I say.

She smiles weakly and closes her eyes. "Thanks," she says.

Olivia is still sleeping at seven-thirty, which I'm now making Owen's bedtime.

"Okay, Owen, how about you show me how you brush your teeth?"

"That's boring," he says. "Let's play Chutes and Ladders instead."

"Make you a deal. You put your pajamas on and brush your teeth, and then we'll play Chutes and Ladders."

"Is Olivia going to play with us?"

"Yeah, I don't think so."

Owen does a minimalist job on his teeth and appears in Batman pajamas. Then he schools me in Chutes and Ladders.

"You're not very lucky, are you?" Owen says after beating me three times.

"Maybe not with Chutes and Ladders, but I got to meet you, didn't I? That's pretty lucky, isn't it?

Owen perks up. "It is. And Olivia's your girlfriend. That's lucky too!"

"She's not exactly my girlfriend. Not yet, anyway," I whisper.

"Oh." Owen looks deflated. "Tomorrow she'll be your girlfriend?"

"You're right," I say. "There's always tomorrow." I look over at Olivia, huddled under the blanket. "Now, come on, champ, let's get you tucked in to bed. Do you need your Spider-Man blanket back?"

Owen seems torn. "I can use my Batman blanket," he says.

"I'll be sure to put this one back in your room when she wakes up."

Owen looks relieved. "I'm Batman!" he says. He runs off to his bedroom, cape flying behind him.

"Don't forget the nightlight," he says as I tuck him in.

"Sure thing. Hey, Owen, do you think maybe you could try not to mention to your parents that I was here tonight?"

"Lying not good. Lying bad," he says, clutching a stuffed Batman.

Great, Jacob. You can be responsible for teaching this kid to lie. "It wouldn't be exactly lying, just leaving something out. So Olivia wouldn't get in trouble for falling asleep."

"In trouble because boyfriend here."

I sigh. "I'm not her boyfriend, remember?"

"Tomorrow," he says.

"Right, maybe tomorrow she'll be my girlfriend."

"I won't tell."

I pull the Batman blanket up to his chin. "Thanks, bud."

Back in the living room, I crouch on the floor in front of the couch. "Olivia?" I say, putting my hand on her shoulder.

Her eyes fly open.

"I'm awake," she says, sitting up and rubbing her eyes. "But I'm still exhausted."

"Is everything okay? You seem to be cold a lot...and tired." I plop down on the couch next to her.

She shrugs. "I must be coming down with something."

"Maybe you should see a doctor."

Olivia frowns then leans her head against me.

"You don't have a doctor phobia, do you?"

"What, like your fear of enclosed spaces?" She twists around to look at me, her eyes dancing.

"That wouldn't have been an issue if you'd have kept moving in the tunnel like you were supposed to. And now you're just changing the subject." I place my hands on Olivia's shoulders and massage her neck.

"Thanks, that feels good. Okay, so I'm not a fan of doctors. But really, I think it's probably just a combination of people over-air conditioning and me not getting enough sleep."

"Don't tell me you're staying up too late because of homework? Please tell me that it's because you can't wait until the next time you see me."

"You'd like that, wouldn't you? Maybe it's a little bit of both."

"Hmm," I say, unconvinced. I don't think it's either of those two reasons, but I decide not to push the issue. Which doesn't stop me from worrying.

Thirty-One

OLIVIA

I sit on the balcony outside of my dad's office and look out over the backyard, journal in lap, pen in hand, writing about the voices. And about Jacob

My dad also kept a journal of sorts. Really it was just a notebook full of lists. It's the one stuffed in the cushion of the burgundy chair. Alongside the book I bought on schizophrenia. I found it when we were at my dad's apartment after he died. My mom found it first and put it on the trash heap. But I found it second and smuggled it out of there and kept it. I couldn't read all the words at first, but as the years went on, I understood them all too well.

My dad's notebook has lists like: feed baby, change diaper, play with her. I guess it's kind of weird that my dad needed a list to know that he was supposed to play with me, but I like to pretend that he put "play with her" on the list because he loved me and wanted to remind himself what was important in life.

My voices have never told me to do anything that was bad or that

I didn't want to do. But a few pages past the list about my care and feeding, there's another list in my dad's notebook. It just says *Kill wife and daughter.* And on the page after that there's a drawing of a gun. The thing about my dad was that I never saw this side of him. I saw the side of him that read the same page of Babar over and over and that listened to the people inside of marbles, but I never saw the side of him that wrote *Kill wife and daughter.*

Okay, so that's not completely true, just mostly true.

Thirty-Two

JACOB

ick says something to me in art class.

"Mmm." I'm trying to focus on the face that I'm sketching. Shit. The eyes need to be closer together. I grab an eraser.

Nick spins around and around in his chair. "For after we're done playing?"

"Mmm."

"Hello? Earth to Jacob! I just asked you if you have a date for after we're done playing at the dance? Since when is art more important than talking about hot women?" He peers over at my sketch pad. "Whoa, da Vinci! You've got some pretty fine sketching skills. But why waste your talent on old men? Why not concentrate on your Mona Lisa? Girls dig that shit."

"You think so?" He doesn't get it. It's not that I want to draw that old man. It's just the only way I can get him out of my head.

"I know so. Who is that dude, anyway? He your grandpa or something?"

"You don't recognize him?"

"Should I?"

"I don't know. I think I saw him around town somewhere." Make that in a dream, standing on the edge of a cliff, jumping.

"Hate to break it to you, but this place isn't that small. We don't all know each other like you did in that Podunk town you're from in Michigan."

I give up on the drawing and set the pencil down. "It can come in handy sometimes, you know."

"What, you know the sheriff?"

I shrug my shoulders.

"You're shittin' me!" He slaps me on the back. "You little devil! What mischief did you get yourself out of?"

"I might have been a little drunk when my friend drove us into a tree."

It takes him a minute to figure it out. "And this sheriff you know—he might have forgotten to charge you with minor in possession?"

I shrug again.

"You lucky bastard!"

I grin with him even though I don't feel so lucky anymore. I'd gladly take ten minor in possessions if I could just get my headaches and fucked-up dreams to go away.

"So who else you got in this book of yours? Please tell me you have the sheriff!"

"No sheriff. This sketchbook has nothing but crap." I'm not ready to share the complete version of Faces from Whacked-Out Cliff-Diving Dreams just yet. Make that ever. I can't even believe I brought it here. I close it and slide it under my English book. "The answer to your question is yes."

Nick squints his eyes. "What question was that?"

"You asked if I had a date for the dance."

"Nice! Who is she?"

"Olivia Anderson."

Nick whistles. "You don't waste any time, do you? That girl is something special. Law abiding too. You better not blow it, dude. Cops around here have pretty good memories."

"I'll keep that in mind. So who are you taking?" I ask.

"I'm keeping my options open."

"In other words, the girl you wanted to take said no?"

"No, I haven't asked the girl I want to take yet." Nick spins around on his stool.

"Well, what are you waiting for?"

He sighs. "Maybe for her to stop drooling over some other guy?"

"Ouch. Any end in sight?"

Nick stops himself from spinning by grabbing hold of the table. "I'm expecting reality to hit her at the dance itself."

"So you're going to swoop in for a slow dance or dedicate a song to her?"

"We shall see, my man. We shall see."

Thirty-Three

OLIVIA

*He's here," my mom shouts.

I stop fussing with my hair and make my way down the stairs. The last thing I need is my mom talking Jacob's ear off.

"Good evening, Mrs. Anderson," Jacob says, handing her a bouquet of flowers, the kind that are dyed in vibrant rainbow colors. "These are for you. I'm Jacob, by the way."

"Nice to meet you, Jacob. Come on in. And thank you for the flowers. They're lovely."

Jacob catches my eye on the stairs and smiles. He's rocking the whole jeans and T-shirt with a jacket look.

"Hi, Olivia," he says. "You look beautiful." When I get to the bottom step, he hands me a red rose.

"Thanks," I say.

"Would you like to have a seat and..."

"I think we're just going to head out, Mom," I say before she can start

116

pulling up baby pictures on Facebook.

Once we've cleared the porch, I hold up my keys. "Want to drive?"

"Whoa. Visitation rights on the Jeep. Are you sure?"

"I think you might actually be gentler with her than I am."

"That's for sure," he mutters under his breath.

"Watch it, or I'll change my mind."

Jacob holds up his hands in mock surrender, then opens the door for me. I climb in the passenger seat and breathe in the sweet smell of my rose.

"So is this our first real date?" Jacob asks.

"What, you don't count laser tag? I'm hurt."

"I guess we can count that if you want. It beats my parents' first date. My dad took my mom to the grocery store to get ant traps."

I laugh. "I have to agree. That bar is pretty low."

I bring the rose to my nose again and breathe in. I love that smell. Only...I feel cold. I roll up the window, hoping that's the problem.

It's not. I'm chilled the whole car ride, but I can see beads of sweat on Jacob's forehead, so I hold myself back from turning on the heat.

Once we get out of the Jeep, the chill evaporates. Jacob walks me in, then leaves to go get ready with his band. They play the first set.

"This song isn't bad—for country," Julia shouts. "Who sings it?"

"Thomas Rhett."

They don't play the slow song from that day on the balcony, but I'm okay with that because I wouldn't want to dance to it without Jacob.

When they finish their set, Jacob runs his fingers through his hair and scans the crowd. He sees me and waves, then works his way over. "This must be one of your birds," he says, pointing to a floating crane and laughing. "Since it's crooked and all."

"You better watch it," I say. "Or you'll have to find someone else to dance with." The moment I say it, I want to take it back. There are plenty of girls here who would dance with Jacob.

The music turns slow. Jacob raises his eyebrows and slips his arms behind my back. A little self-consciously, I put mine around his neck.

Julia floats by with Conrad. Completely mesmerized. Is that how I look?

Jacob presses his cheek against mine. The bit of stubble there scratches, in a good way. He smells of cinnamon and something woodsy, like the pine needles on my favorite hiking trail. As we sway to the music, Jacob's fingers tickle my back.

"Mmm," he whispers. "Your hair smells good. What is that, vanilla?"

"Vanilla raspberry."

"I guess you really do like raspberries."

"Mmm hmm."

Tingles travel from my fingers to my toes. When is he going to kiss me?

The song rolls along, and then it's over. A fast song is up next. Reluctantly, I drop my arms.

"I've got to get a drink," says Jacob. "Come with me?"

I nod, and we snake our way to the punch bowl. The drink is orange with clouds of pink floaties. Jacob takes a cup and drains it.

"Wow, that's way too sweet," he says. "I need a drinking fountain. Where's the closest?"

"This way." Jacob follows me out the side door of the gym. The door closes behind us, muffling the pounding music.

"Around the corner," I say.

Jacob takes a long drink of water as I lean against a locker. Sweat trickles down my back.

Cupping some of the water in his hand, Jacob splashes it on his face. Then he cups some more and flicks it at me.

It actually feels good, so I barely flinch. He does it again. This time he gets my hair.

"Oh no you don't," I say. "Not the hair. The hair is off limits." I turn on the drinking fountain and stick my hand in the stream to divert it toward Jacob's face. He just laughs and steps backward. I narrow my eyes, cup one hand, fill, and toss.

"So you want to fight?" Jacob says. I fill my hand again. Before I can toss it, Jacob grabs my wrist, and the water runs down my arm. I reach back with my other hand and turn the water fountain on. Jacob easily wrenches my hand free and pushes me gently against the locker. He holds my hands behind my back. "Now what are you going to do?" he asks.

"I think the better question is, what are you going to do?"

Instead of answering, Jacob lets go of my hands and pushes the hair out of my eyes. Then he puts his hands on either side of my face and presses his lips against mine. The music in the background fades away, my whole body pulses with something electric, and my fear of the voices floats away, if only for a few moments.

Thirty-Four

OLIVIA

*T*here's a stone path in my backyard that weaves from the lilacs, which aren't blooming any longer, to the hydrangeas, which are. Midway through the path are the ferns, nestled under a canopy of trees, and a porch swing in a metal frame. I love this spot. I take a deep breath and open the box of photos that Samantha's mom gave me for the yearbook tribute.

No voices. At least not yet.

I pick up a photo labeled *first day of school*. A lop-sided grin and a missing tooth. Birthday party at a bounce house, second grade. I am there with her, my arm around her shoulder. We are jumping high in the air, laughing. Life was good. Third grade, family vacation to the Grand Canyon. She looks so small next to the vast backdrop behind her.

The memories march on. I pick out pictures, laughing at some, crying at others. I choose the best of the best, then I go inside and scan them.

Afterward I return to the stone path that I once skipped along with my friend and settle back into the swing with my laptop. There I lay out the life of my old friend on two pages with overlapping photos and a quote that I saw on her bedroom wall: *Live every moment as if it were your last.*

Then I hit Save and close the lid to my computer before I hear a voice that no longer belongs in this world.

Thirty-Five

JACOB

On Tuesday, as I'm walking Olivia home past the park, she says, "I just love parks. Reminds me of being a kid, you know?"

All too well. "Uh-huh," I say.

The day my brother disappeared, I had been hiding in a green plastic tunnel on a play structure. I scan the equipment now. No tunnel here. I take a deep breath. A three-year-old boy is running around buzzing like a bee. A girl in a red jumper is scooping sand into another kid's hair. And then I see a kid with blond hair like my brother's and he's running and I want to stop him and I want to hug him and I want him to be my brother and I want it to be that day again, only this time I'll keep my eyes open.

"You okay?" asks Olivia. "I was going to suggest the swings, but you look a little sick."

"Nah, I'm fine. Swings are great."

She smiles, and her hair bounces as she runs for a swing. I run after her.

There's only one kid on the set of four swings. Just as Olivia plants herself on a swing, he takes off, leaving it swinging by itself. I ignore the weight forming at the bottom of my stomach and the choking sensation in my throat, and take over the abandoned swing. Olivia pumps her legs and touches the sky with her feet. I just dangle there with what must be a stupid grin on my face, and I watch her leaning back, her long hair swirling in the wind.

"This is fun, but I think it's making me a little seasick," Olivia says, slowing down. Her swing loses its rhythm and moves side to side, her knees touching mine.

She jumps off the swing. "I guess you'll have to push me then," I say.

She looks a bit doubtful. "Don't worry," I say. "I'll help." I push off and pump my legs, and as I glide back past the dusty pit, Olivia pushes my back with a grunt.

"I can't be that hard to push!" But when I come back around, Olivia is doubled over with laughter. I jump off the swing and grab her hand. "Come on. Let's check out that bridge thing."

Thirty-Six

OLIVIA

I like the feel of Jacob's hand in mine as he leads me over to the swaying bridge. I climb up and run back and forth on the planks a few times. "This reminds me of a haunted house with those crazy shifting floors from when I was a kid. Try that in the dark when you're six."

I plunk myself down in the middle of the bridge. Jacob sits next to me and puts his hand on my knee. I lean my head against his shoulder. "I'm super cold."

"I take it you still haven't seen a doctor? Because it's actually pretty warm out right now."

"Not yet."

And then I hear it. It's super quiet, like a whisper. The voice sounds like it's coming from Jacob, but I know it can't be because it's not his voice. And besides, Jacob's lips aren't moving. It's a young boy's voice. The same voice I heard at Owen's house and in the cave.

Ready or not.

I shake my head, as if that could make it go away, make it stop.

Ready or not.

I laugh, and then I realize that this is exactly what my dad did with the Babar book. He laughed. It must have been the voices that made him laugh. Like they make me laugh. And I'm scared and repulsed, but only at myself, and I feel like I'm going to be sick.

I close my eyes and wait for the feeling to pass. The words swirl in my head. Soft. Childlike. Almost sad. But soothing. As I wait, Jacob's lips brush mine. Soft. Warm. Sensual. My lips tingle as the kiss deepens. Jacob wraps his arms around me and pulls me closer until I can feel the pounding of his heart against my chest. I kiss him back, feeling more alive than ever before.

Ready...

Or not...

The voice gets louder and fills my head, and for a minute I almost lose it. But finally the voice just swirls right up and out of my mind like a funnel cloud on its way to heaven. Just like that, it's gone, and I'm left with the cinnamon taste of Jacob's tongue and the scratch of his stubble and his strong arms wrapped around me, heating my body from the outside in, until I can't understand how I could have been cold.

Thirty-Seven

OLIVIA

One day when I was seven, my dad picked me up from school. This was kind of unusual on account of the restraining order and all. But my seven-year-old self didn't know anything about restraining orders, and even if I did, I would have gladly gotten in the car with him because my dad was FUN, even if he did listen to the people who live in marbles and laugh about elephants getting on elevators.

And fun is what we had, at least at first. We drove all night and the whole next day from Pennsylvania to Florida, and we listened to sad songs on the radio because my dad loved sad songs, and since sad songs made him happy, they made me happy too. We ate fast food, which was fine with me because what kid doesn't like the toy that comes with the Happy Meal? When we got to Florida, I thought we were going to Disney World, and I couldn't wait to take the safari boat ride that Julia had told me about.

But when we got to Florida, we went to the beach, which would have been okay except it was November and midnight. It wasn't that cold, but it was definitely dark. My dad took my hand and dragged me up and down the beach and said, "Isn't Disney World great?" And I started to cry because I knew this wasn't Disney World, but I had a tiny hope that maybe my dad would still take me to the real Disney World.

Eventually my dad did get tired of his fake Disney World, so we got back in the car and listened to some more really sad songs and drove some more. And we got to this place that my dad said was home. There was no electricity, so we had to use flashlights. I got a flashlight of my very own to take up the cobwebbed stairs to a place my dad called my bedroom. In my bedroom, there was a sleeping bag on the floor but no pillow, but I didn't care because I was so very tired. I crawled in that bag that smelled like rotten bananas, and I closed my eyes and went to sleep.

I was so tired I probably would have kept sleeping until well past noon the next day, but instead when I woke up, it was still dark. I wanted so much to go back to sleep, but a little girl kept calling my name. *Olivia! Come outside!* I tried to cover my ears, but it wasn't working, and it was SO HOT inside the sleeping bag. Finally I got up and turned on my little flashlight—only it didn't work nearly as good as it had before because the room looked all cloudy and I couldn't even really figure out where the door was. That's when I started coughing, and I was getting dizzy from spinning around, so finally I just sank back down on top of the sleeping bag. I thought again about going back to sleep, but then that little girl started up again, so I started crawling around, and I crawled until I bumped into the doorframe.

And then I saw the FIRE. Big orange flames, and little ones too, and sparks hitting the ceiling, and then a little spark jumped into my room and onto the sleeping bag and pretty soon I knew there was no way I could ever go back to my sleeping bag. So I found the stairs because of the little sparks dancing all around, and I went down them as the railing turned into a jelly volcano. And the whole time I shouted *Daddy!* He never heard me, I guess, because the only answer I got was from the little girl and her voice just kept getting louder and louder, so I went outside to tell her to be quiet so I could hear my daddy.

But when I got outside, she wasn't there, and even though I called to her, she never answered. And my arm hurt so very bad. I tried to go back in the house to find my daddy and the little girl, only I couldn't find the door because the front of the house all blended into one big wall of fire. I wanted to sit on the porch and wait for them to come out, but the wall of fire pushed me out past the porch, which pretty soon disappeared too, and nobody ever came out of that house. When the fire department finally showed up, I screamed at them to go in and find my daddy and the little girl. They did finally find my daddy, but not before the fire had taken all the life from that house. But there was no little girl. Not in the house and not in the neighborhood, because there wasn't any neighborhood. What my dad decided to make our home was an abandoned farmhouse, miles from anyone else.

That little girl's voice was the first voice I heard that wasn't real. No one, not even my mom, thought twice about me hearing that voice and what it might mean. But that's because I never told them how loud the voice was or how sure I was of it. I never told them because I knew what they would think if I ever told about a voice that wasn't there. They would think I believed that people lived in marbles too. And this is how I got the scar on my arm, because the fire burned it, and though it looks a lot better than it did, it still looks like an arm that's been burned by a fire.

And even though I wanted to believe it was an accident, and I did believe it was an accident for many years, I know it wasn't.

Thirty-Eight

OLIVIA

When I get in the Jeep Saturday morning, I mean to drive to the mall, where I told my mom I'd be, but I just can't. I need the calm and the peace that I can only get one place. The woods.

I make a last-minute right turn, taking the curve a little too fast.

Do I call her? Tell her where I'm going?

I locate my phone, which flew over the passenger seat during that last turn. Too far to reach.

Let's see. *Hey, Mom. You know how I said I was going to the mall? Slight change of plans. I'm headed to my favorite trail. You know, the one with the dirt parking lot that no one's ever at?*

Um, no. Even with no serial killer on the loose, my mom's not a fan of me going there on my own.

Seriously though, that trail is hard to find when you know where it is. Let alone if you're some guy from Ohio looking to snatch a teenage girl. From my perspective the mall's a lot more dangerous.

But not my mom's.

I swallow my guilt, take some more turns a little too fast, and drive.

When I get to the end of an unmarked road, my Jeep is the only one in the so-called parking lot. I climb out of the car, hit the lock button, and breathe in the crisp, cool air, a touch colder than normal for September. As I walk, my legs tingle, and a feeling of calm settles over me.

Hello, tall trees; hello, sweet scent of pine; hello, chipmunk running across the path and deer standing frozen on a blanket of leaves.

Goodbye, sadness; goodbye, worries; goodbye, voices that don't belong.

With each step, I'm a bit more free.

A half hour passes, maybe more.

And then it starts.

Olivia!

No.

Olivia!

Shh!

Olivia!

Samantha's voice. Can't you just leave me alone?

Olivia!

I stop and look up, even though I know damn well the voice is coming from my head.

Olivia!

One of those stupid yellow birds with the black cap is perched on a branch right above me.

Olivia!

Sure enough, the voice seems to be coming from the bird. I wave my arms, hoping to scare it away. As it flaps its small wings and flies off, I follow its progress with my eyes. The funny thing is that the farther away the bird gets, the louder the voice is, until I can't see the bird anymore, but I still hear Samantha's voice. I follow it.

Now off the path, I hold my hands in front of my face to protect it from twigs. My ankles smart from the scratches caused by brambles, and clumps of burs stick to my clothes. Samantha's voice is no longer overhead with the bird. It's low to the ground, full and vibrant. And it's coming from right in front of me, from the river. I stop abruptly, teetering on the edge.

Olivia!

The whole river vibrates with Samantha's voice. I want to slip into it, even though I know it's stupid because I'm wearing tennis shoes and shorts and not a swimming suit, and it's September, not July, and the water is going to be icy. I sway on the edge, considering my move.

Olivia!

The water draws me in like a snake charmer. Its chill shocks me, even though I'm expecting it. My tennis shoes squish against the muck at the bottom. I find myself wading in deeper and deeper, and the water buzzes as Samantha's voice fills me. The buzzing feeling is so mesmerizing, I almost like it. No. I do like it—a lot.

As the buzz flows through my body, I sink deeper and deeper into the water until it covers my head. And then I spread my arms out, and I float. I flip on my back, and I laugh. The current starts to pull me downstream. At first it's gentle and I don't mind, but then it tugs harder, until all of a sudden I realize that I'm in the middle of the river and I can't touch the bottom.

I swallow some water, and my heart seems to tumble around in my chest. My feet feel weighed down by the tennis shoes, and I think I'm going to drown. Samantha's voice has stopped, the buzzing in the water has stopped, and I can't figure out why I ever thought this would be a good idea.

I spit out water and gulp a big breath of air. Flailing my arms, I struggle to reach the shore. The current keeps tugging me, faster and faster now, and I grasp at branches as I pass them, but all I end up with is scratches on my arms, which I can't feel because the water has numbed them, which could be why I can't grab hold of anything.

I grab a log that's jutting out and bob there for a bit. I think about leaning back and going under the log and just floating away. I'm so tired and that sounds so easy, so I consider it, but only for a minute. Then I pull myself bit by bit back to the shore until I'm nearly there. My knees touch the bottom. I grab at the bank and mud comes loose in my hand and I grab again and I get more dirt along with something else. As I crawl back onto the shore, I look at the something else.

It's a necklace.

I dip it back in the water to wash the mud from the pendant.

A butterfly.

It's still pretty, even after all that soaking in the river. I like the feel of the chain between my fingers, with all of those links woven together. Should I keep it? It's just costume jewelry, so it's not like it's worth anything. Besides, it's not like there's a lost and found for rivers. It's long enough that I can pull it over my head without opening the clasp. Which I do. And then I stand up and walk back to the Jeep, my toes squishing water out of the soles of my shoes with every step.

Thirty-Nine

JACOB

On Saturday around noon, I grab an Asiago bagel from the counter and slice it in half. My mom's scrambling eggs at the stove. "You want me to fry you up an egg for that? There's bacon and cheese in the fridge if you want to make a sandwich."

"Sure, thanks."

While the egg cooks, I text Olivia to see if she wants to do anything. Then I continue reading a James Patterson novel that I found in the living room earlier in the week.

"You always were a reader when you were younger," my mom says. "It's good to see you keeping it up."

"I'm actually not much of a reader anymore." I was too busy partying with Ricky and company. Not that you would know it now. I haven't been to a single party since I've been here. I actually got invited to a few, I just wasn't feeling it. Pathetic.

The bacon sizzles as it's dropped into the pan. My stomach rumbles as the smells of bacon and eggs meld together. I stick my nose back in the book, and I don't resurface until something bumps my hand, making me jump. It's just the sandwich plate. My mom managed to toast the bagel and assemble the whole thing without me even noticing.

"Thanks." I set the book down and take a bite. "Wow, this is delicious."

My mom beams and doesn't even comment on my talking with my mouth full. "Glad you like it." She stabs her scrambled eggs with her fork as I return to the book.

"Your dad called last night. He was wondering why you haven't been returning his calls."

"Tell him he should text."

"You need to stop blaming your dad for sending you here. Your dad and I made that decision together."

"He doesn't need me, I don't need him."

"You know that's not why you're here."

Goddamn it! "Right. It's because I'm a fuck-up and a screw-up. That's why I'm here." I stand up, knocking my chair over. This is the part where she's supposed to say that I'm here because she wants me to be. Because she needs me. But of course she doesn't say it. She'll never say it. Never mean it. "I'm going for a walk." I throw my napkin down and stomp off.

"Jacob, your sandwich!"

I stomp back into the kitchen, pick up the chair I knocked over, snatch my sandwich, and storm back out.

The part that hurts so much, the part that makes me so angry, is not the thought that I've been sent here because I screwed up with Ricky and because of all the partying and the drinking. It's the thought that my dad doesn't need me anymore. Even though my mom denied it, I know that's the real reason I'm here. My dad has his new wife. I'm just extra baggage.

Although I haven't heard back from her yet, my feet take me to

Olivia's house. I shuffle up her front porch steps and ring the bell.

No answer.

I'm just about to leave when Olivia pulls into the driveway, gets out of her Jeep, and ambles toward me. She's walking like a zombie, and she's totally drenched, even her tennis shoes.

"A little chilly to be going for a swim, isn't it?"

Olivia shakes her head as if she just now noticed me on her porch. "Oh, yeah. I kind of fell in the river while I was hiking."

"Yikes! Are you okay? How did that happen?"

"I was near the water and then…well, I guess I must have tripped on a root or something…"

"Nice necklace," I say.

"Isn't it? I found it by the river."

"I was just coming to see if you wanted to do something, but I can come back later."

"No, it's okay. Come on in. I just need to take a shower."

Inside, Olivia pries off her shoes and leaves them on the rug. Then she heads up the stairs. "Come on up. You can wait in my room while I shower."

I follow Olivia up the stairs to her room, where she rustles around in her drawers and pulls out some dry clothes. The room is big and open and airy, and light shines brightly in the windows. I find a bean bag chair and sink into it. "I'll be back in a few minutes," she says.

I nod and adjust the lumps in the bean bag chair until they're more comfortable. Olivia really has a calm vibe going here, with posters of waterfalls and rainforests, and…*Shit.* She has a poster of a canyon, not unlike the one in my dream. Nope. I'm not letting one little picture spoil this day. No way. I close my eyes and settle into the beanbag, and pretty soon the sound of the shower nudges out the image of the canyon.

After some time the water stops. At the end of the hallway, a door creaks open, and feet shuffle down the hallway.

"Oh, right. I told you to wait here, didn't I? I was a little out of it, I think." I open my eyes. Olivia is in the doorway, wearing leggings and a long-sleeve shirt that clings in all the right places. The scent of apples wafts from her skin, her hair shiny wet.

My mouth goes dry. I stand and stare at her, and I have this overwhelming urge to kiss her. Only, I know I better not, because here we are alone in her bedroom and my every nerve is firing. "We should probably go down to the living room," I say.

She nods. I walk to the door and I mean to go right past her, only first I lean over and kiss her lightly. Her lips taste like apples too. When she doesn't push me away, I do it again, this time a little deeper. Then I push her against the wall, but gently, and I pick her up. She's light.

Forty

OLIVIA

He picks me up. I can't help but think of the fire. Of the fireman who carried me away from the house. But it's Jacob who sets me down on the bed. My bed. I'm not seven. I'm seventeen. I have this feeling like I'm being scorched. Only it's not by the fire. It's with Jacob's eyes. I try to think about the river and how I have to tell someone that I'm going crazy, just like my dad, but I don't want to, I just want to forget it all, I just want to be here with Jacob.

Jacob lies on top of me. *Oh God.* He covers my lips with his lips, and I feel like I'm melting into him. He groans and buries his mouth in my neck, and everything I've been worrying about slips away. I breathe in his scent that is all boy and slide my fingers underneath his shirt and down his back. His hips twitch, and the movement sends ripples of pleasure tingling through my legs. I slide the sides of his shirt up until I can slip it over his head. I kiss him again and run my fingers over his chest.

I stop thinking. I stop thinking about anything at all. I want him. I want this. I—

Oh God. Footsteps on the stairs. Oh shit. "That's my…" Another delicious sensation rocks my body. "My mom's home. She's coming up the stairs."

Jacob freezes, his body pressing down so completely against mine that I can barely think. I don't want to think. I want to just…

He slides slowly off of me, taking one more wicked look at me. "Now what?"

"The closet."

"Don't tell me to hide in the closet," he whispers at the same time.

I give him an apologetic shrug. "At least it's a walk-in," I say. Unusual in a Victorian house. Definitely not original.

"Great," he says, looking less than thrilled. "Can I at least have something to read?"

Full panic is starting to set in. "Something to read?" I shove a magazine in his hands and push him into the closet.

"Ten signs a guy might like you?" he says. "Ooh, there's a quiz. Can I have a pen?"

"Shh!" I say frantically. "No pen!" Footsteps move down the hallway.

"Hello!" calls my mom. I look in the mirror to make sure everything looks normal. God, my hair is a wreck. I grab my brush and attack the tangles.

There's a tap on the door, and I lose control of the hairbrush. It nearly takes out my mom as she opens the door.

"I just got back from the grocery store. How was the mall?"

"Great. It was great."

"You're not coming down with something, are you? You look a little flushed."

Oh my God. That's because I was seconds away from having sex.

"I am a little tired. I think I'll just lie down for a few minutes." In my closet. With the hottest guy to hit Ridgeview in a decade or so.

She puts her hand on my forehead. "You do that," she says, all concerned. Now I really feel like shit. But not so bad that I don't open the closet door the second she's gone.

Oh God. His bare chest is as hot as ever.

Forty-One

JACOB

When Olivia opens the door, I see the flush her mom was talking about. It's sexy as hell. I pull her into the closet and clutch her close to me. Then I ease her on top of me, on top of a pile of high-heeled shoes. One pokes my back. I don't even care. Or at least not enough to stop.

"You've got to get out of here," she whispers in my ear.

"Mmm," I say, putting my hands on her butt and drawing her closer. She draws her breath in sharply, and I groan as quietly as possible.

"You've got to leave before my mom notices you're in the closet," she hisses. Her mentioning her mom is almost as effective as a cold shower, except that her body is still pressing against mine in a way that's sucking all the reason out of my brain.

"Right. Must go now," I say, drawing the words out as long as possible to keep her on top of me.

"I'll see if the coast is clear," she says and then goes in for a deep, mind-blowing kiss.

"Uh-huh," I say, my thoughts a shivering mess of Jell-O.

Then she gets off of me and she's gone, and I'm left on the closet floor, trying to hold on to the feeling of her body pulsing against mine.

She waves me out of the closet, finger over her lips.

I can't resist. I move her finger away and kiss her.

"Olivia?" There's a tap on the door a second before it opens. Olivia shoves me in the corner and grabs the door.

"Have you seen my tennis shoes?" asks her mom.

"I think they're in your closet," Olivia says, boxing her mom out of the room.

"No, I just checked there. They must be downstairs."

"I'm pretty sure they're not. Check under your bed. I'll look downstairs."

"Aren't you sweet?" says her mom, her voice fading down the hallway.

Olivia gestures wildly for me to escape out of the room. I follow her downstairs. I can't help grinning at the panic in her eyes.

"You're impossible," she hisses, shooing me out. "Call me later."

"Most definitely," I answer.

Forty-Two

JACOB

My mom has always been a movie buff, and she still has a ton of DVDs junking up her bookshelves, even though I've tried to explain to her that she really needs to go digital. Her collection is heavy on foreign films, musicals, and Nicolas Sparks, but I finally find a *Star Trek* movie on the top shelf. I pull it out, knocking another film to the ground. It's a home movie. Wow. I haven't seen one of these since…well, since before Dad and I moved out. Before I can think too much about it, I pop the DVD out of its case and slide it in the player.

Ben in his highchair fills the screen. "Juh, Juh, Juh," he's saying, pointing at a younger version of me. My mom used to think it was so cute that because he couldn't say my whole name, he would call me by the sound of the first letter, but I hated it. And now…now I just wish I could hear him say anything at all.

"Jacob?" My mom is calling from the kitchen. I hit pause, and it seems like Ben is staring right at me.

"In here."

Her footsteps stop abruptly in the doorway.

"Oh. You're watching these," she says. She takes one step backward as if she's going to back right on out of here, but then she grabs the doorframe and propels herself into the room. She sits on the couch, a gap the size of the Mississippi between us. "They're hard to watch," she says.

"Yeah. I miss him like crazy."

"I miss him too," she says. "But that's not the only reason they're hard to watch."

"It's not?"

She shakes her head. "I should say, they *were* hard to watch. They were hard to watch because you're in them, Jacob. And you weren't here."

"And whose fault was that?" I snap.

She doesn't answer. She just bites her lip and stares at the TV. *Damn it.* I can't do this. I stand up, ready to bolt.

My mom sucks in her breath. Her hand jumps up and covers her mouth. Her eyes are locked on the TV.

Ben's playing with his favorite stuffed animal, a fairly plump blue rabbit.

"He loved that ratty old thing," my mom says, her voice shaking.

"Yeah, what was its name?" I ask, even though I know the answer.

"Fuzzy," she says.

"That's right. Fuzzy." Ben had Fuzzy in his arms the day we played hide-and-seek.

"I wouldn't be here if it weren't for Ricky driving into that tree, you know."

She tears her eyes away from the TV and studies me. "Thank him for me the next time you talk to him."

"Seriously?"

"First tell him that if he ever puts you in danger again, I'll kill him myself. Then you can thank him."

"I think I'll pass." I sit back down on the couch and put my feet up on the coffee table. I sneak a glance at my mom out of the corner of my eye, waiting for her to tell me to move them. I can see her looking sideways as well. Her lips twitch, but she doesn't say anything.

"Don't you have to work?" I prod.

"In a bit."

Ben is onscreen twirling himself in circles.

"You know what happens next, don't you?" she asks.

"Yeah." *Three, two, one.* He's so dizzy he falls to the floor. His eyes are closed, his body's still, and he's got a big grin on his face.

Then the camera fades to black.

Forty-Three

OLIVIA

If I could, I would write a book about my dad and his whole life before he was crazy. But I barely know anything about him. His parents are both dead and he was an only child, and I'm an only child and my mom won't really talk much about him, so all I know are the crazy parts. Maybe instead I'll write a science-fiction book, and it'll be about the people who live inside of marbles. Because I think they would like to have their story told.

Forty-Four

JACOB

~~~∾⃝⃝∾~~~

I'm sitting at the kitchen table eating breakfast and sketching some woman's face on a random piece of paper instead of in my sketchbook. Milk dribbles off my chin and splashes on my paper. I wipe it with my sleeve, but I'm still left with a wet spot. No matter. The picture's done. That's out of my system. It's almost like drawing is my new addiction. Why drink beer when you can draw? I've got to tell that one to Ricky. He'll laugh his ass off. On second thought, I better not. He'd probably round up the old crew and fly in for an intervention. Or more likely, cross state lines fully intoxicated.

Speaking of interventions, someone really needs to tell my mom to stop leaving her work files all over the kitchen table. Isn't this shit confidential or something? I open the top file on the stack, if you can call that Leaning Tower of Pisa a stack.

James Callaghan.

Holy shit. This must be one of the Sweet Dreams Strangler suspects. One god-awful mug shot. Juvenile record a mile long. Childhood trauma. For a second I almost feel sorry for him. Then I think about the girls he might have killed.

I spread the papers out and read through them one by one. There goes another drop of milk. *Damn it! Be more careful, dude.*

"Morning!"

What the...

I nearly knock over the entire bowl of cereal as I scramble to shove all of Mom's papers back in the folder. Straightening the edges the best I can, I toss the file on top of the stack. I grab my cereal bowl and dump it in the sink as my mom enters the room.

"Someone's anxious to get to school," she says.

I grunt.

"Big test?"

I wouldn't know.

My mom's grinning. "Or is it the new girlfriend?"

I almost smile. Who says moms aren't cool? "Olivia is planning on coming over after dinner tonight. We have some studying to do. Is that okay?"

"Fine. And don't forget to call your dad tonight. It's Sophie—I mean Sophia's birthday."

"See, it *is* hard to remember her name!"

She laughs. "Actually, it's not. But I'm the ex-wife. I'm not expected to play nice. You, on the other hand, should at least try to be supportive."

Maybe she's right. But I'm still not calling.

Forty-Five

OLIVIA

As I ring the bell on Jacob's porch, the split pea soup I had for dinner rumbles around in my stomach. I hate pea soup. The only reason I ate it was because it was warm. Now I'm wishing I'd skipped it. Jacob's mom lets me in, a dishtowel in her hands.

"Do you need some help with the dishes?"

She smiles. "Thank you but no. I'm just finishing up, and I know you guys have to study. Jacob's in his room. You can go ahead down there."

"Thanks."

She closes the front door behind me and returns to the kitchen.

I continue down the hallway and rap on Jacob's door.

"What is it?" Jacob asks as he opens the door, sounding annoyed.

"Uh…"

"Oh, I thought you were my mom. Sorry."

"I can go get her if you want."

"Nah. You're cuter." He grins, then leans down and kisses me quickly on the lips. "Come on in." He grabs one hand and pulls me into the room, shutting the door firmly, then puts his hands on my cheeks and gives me a better kiss. And another. And another.

I slide my backpack off and let it drop to the ground. Pretty soon his hands are under my shirt and mine are under his, and we're doing this slow dance backwards until my legs hit the side of the bed and I lose my balance. Jacob helps it along, and before I know it, I'm lying on his bed. Jacob plops down next to me. He's laughing, and I'm giggling. I scrunch up higher on the bed so my legs aren't hanging off the side, and my head hits something hard. "Ouch. What's that?" I pull the offending object out from under my head. It's some sort of book. I turn to the side so I can drop it on the ground, but as I do, I notice the cover. It's a sketchbook. "Hey, wait a minute. You draw? Like for real? Not just dolphins on your chem notes?"

Jacob grunts, kissing my neck as I lean over the edge to drop the book on the floor. But first I open the cover and flip through the pages, stopping on a picture of a girl. I lean in for a better look. Jacob tickles me, trying to make me let go. "You don't want to look at that," he says. His fingers trace the outline of my bra, and I almost drop the book, only there's something about that drawing that I have to see. I squirm my way out from under Jacob and take the book with me to a corner of the room. Jacob follows me, trying to yank it out of my hands.

"This is a picture of Samantha," I say. "Why did you draw a picture of her? That's kind of weird, you know. She was my friend."

"I thought you hadn't talked to her in years," Jacob shoots back.

My eyes sting. I turn the pages of the book. "Who are these people? Is that another one of the Sweet Dreams Strangler's victims? Are all of these people dead?"

Jacob sinks back onto the bed and runs his fingers through his hair. "I can explain," he says.

"Explain what? Your obsession with the dead? Your necro–, necro–"

Jacob sighs. "I think the word you're looking for is necrophilia. And I'm not obsessed with dead girls. It's just..."

I flip back to the page with Samantha on it. Then I hear her voice. *Don't give up.*

"No!" This can't be happening again. Why won't it stop? As I put my hands over my ears, Jacob's sketchbook falls to the ground.

Tears trickle down my face. "I'm sorry. I have to go." I grab my backpack by one of the straps. The contents spill everywhere.

"Damn it!" I scoop up my folders and books and stuff everything back inside.

"Olivia, listen, if you'd just let me explain." Jacob puts his hand on my shoulder.

"It's okay. But I really have to go." *You don't really know the whole me. And I'm too afraid to tell you the truth.* I shrug his hand off. "Bye, Jacob."

"Wait!" he calls out as I run down the hall and out of the house, slamming the door behind me.

Forty-Six

JACOB

∞⤜⤛∞

"Jacob? Is everything all right?" My mom pops her head in the door, all perky.

I'm so mad I don't even bother straightening the bedspread to cover for the fact that just moments ago Olivia and I were there making out. Of all things to leave lying around, why did it have to be that stupid sketchpad? Even a condom would have been better. At least that could be explained.

"Yeah. It's all good. Olivia just forgot there was something she had to do at home."

"Oh. Because it sounded like an argument to me."

Where's my dad when I need him? And why isn't there any alcohol in this place? Doesn't the guy my mom's dating ever just want a beer? Doesn't my mom ever want something that will help her forget? How can she stand never once forgetting about Ben?

"Well, it wasn't. And besides, I've got a band rehearsal to get to."

"Now?"

"Yep." I get up and grab my keys, phone, and drumsticks.

"See you." I give her a kiss on the cheek on the way out. Partly because I know she means well. And partly because I'm about to go out and get shit-faced drunk, and I don't want her to get suspicious.

In the truck I skip the texting and just give Nick a call.

"Hello?"

"Hey, it's Jacob. You got any beer? Because I really need to get drunk."

He laughs. "I'll see what I can do. See you in the carriage house in fifteen?"

"The sooner, the better," I say, tearing out of there.

I park on the street at Nick's place, closing the door as quietly as possible, not wanting his parents to find the need to come out and investigate. Light from inside the carriage house spills out from under the side door. Inside I find Nick slouched on a bale of hay, a bottle of beer in hand. I sit down on a bale across from him, and he tosses me a cold one.

"Thanks."

"Sorry, a six pack was all I could manage with the late notice."

"No problem. Much appreciated, dude."

"You sounded pretty riled up. What's got you down?"

There's no way I'm talking to a dude about my creepy-ass drawings. I shrug. "Girl trouble, I guess." I twist off the cap and take a big swig.

"Olivia?"

"Yeah. She got mad and took off." I take another swig. Start tapping my toe.

"You try and call her?"

"Ten times. While driving. She's not answering."

"Text?"

"Just once. Not the kind of thing that can be settled with a text."

"Give her time. She'll come around."

I nod. "That girl you were into finally see the light?"

Nick pulls a straw out of the bale and starts fiddling with it. "Nah."

"Fine pair we are." I get up and tap my fingers lightly on the drum set.

"Go for it. It's not that late."

"That's okay. In the mood I'm in, it would just make the dog next door howl."

Nick chuckles.

"You live here a long time?"

"My whole life. For what it's worth, Olivia seems really into you. She doesn't date much, so that says something, I think."

"Has it got something to do with her scar?"

"Not unless it's on her end. The girl's gorgeous, with or without the scar. Guys ask her out plenty. She just doesn't say yes too often."

"You know how she got the scar?"

"It happened when we were seven. Her dad, who was some kind of crazy, kidnapped her and took her down south. Set fire to the house they were in. Burned himself up. Olivia was lucky to make it out alive."

"What? It must have been an accident, right?"

"Not according to the news stories. They said it was arson. Guy did it himself. 'Course, none of our parents told us that, but enough of us had older siblings who could read the stories on the Internet."

"Shit. That's seriously fucked up. I never would've guessed."

"I know, right? The girl's tough as nails."

The door creaks open. I hope to God it's Olivia. Not that it's possible, since I didn't tell her I was coming here. But still.

"Hey, guys!" It's Katie.

"Hey," Nick and I answer in unison.

"I heard Jacob was feeling down. My brother couldn't make it, so I thought I'd come cheer you up instead."

"Nice of you," I say as she cozies up next to me, putting an arm around my shoulders. Nick tosses her a beer. She leans forward and grabs it with one hand, pulling me with her a bit.

Nick's looking down at his feet, and I swear his face is redder than it was a minute ago.

Shit. This is the girl he was talking about. The one he said he thought was into someone else. And that someone else, I'm guessing, is me.

Nick stands. "You know, I think I'm going to head back in. Just make sure you clean up the empties."

"Wait! Now that you got me cheered back up, I remembered that I promised to take Olivia to the movies. You're not going to make this lady drink alone, are you, Nick?"

Nick looks at me like I've sprouted a horn, and his face grows even redder. I slap him on the shoulder and lean in toward his ear. "Make your move already," I mutter and punch his other shoulder for good measure.

"Haven't you been drinking?" Katie asks. "Should you be driving?"

"Barely half a beer. I'll be fine."

I head for the door, turning around for a wave as I reach it. Nick's taken my place on the hay bale next to Katie. My man.

As I walk out into the night, I realize that I do feel better. As shitty as it is to have Olivia mad at me, the girl's definitely been through worse, and Nick's probably right. If I just give her a little time, she'll come around, and I'll be able to explain…yeah, right. Explain that drawing people, especially dead ones, makes me feel calmer.

I pull out my phone and try to compose a text to Olivia, but I end up erasing everything.

Patience. You can talk to her tomorrow. I take a deep breath, start the truck, and drive. I'm done drinking, but I'm not quite ready to go home, or at least my subconscious isn't, since I'm driving in the opposite direction. This is stupid. My breath probably reeks of beer.

If I get stopped.... But I don't turn around.

I feel around in the glove compartment until I find a pack of gum and stuff a stick in my mouth. It's old and rubbery, but at least it makes me smell like cinnamon. I flip on the radio. It's tuned to a country station, and even though I haven't got the slightest idea who's singing, it makes me think of Olivia, and I smile.

An hour goes by. I'm mellow, at peace.

Holy shit! A throbbing pain spreads from the center of my forehead to my temples and beyond. My left eye feels like it's been stabbed. I slap one hand over it. Headlights from the other cars flash like lightning.

Can't see!

I pull over into a parking lot, wrestle with my phone, and squint so I can text my mom.

Crashing at Nick's.

I let my phone drop and lay my head on the seat.

I close my eyes, rub my temples with my fingers, and pray for the agony to pass.

Forty-Seven

JACOB

*I*t's happening again. The dream. When I see the cliff, I start running in the opposite direction, but a strong, tornado-esque wind is whipping, blowing dust in my eyes, pushing me backward, closer and closer to the crowd at the edge of the cliff, until I'm there, in the midst of them, the only one facing away from the cliff.

I stand there for what feels like hours. I shuffle my feet. I'm thirsty, and I just want to leave, to get out of here, but every time I try to take a step forward, the wind slaps me back into place. Never hard enough to send me over the edge, only hard enough to ensure that I'm stuck here. Finally, I turn around and sit down, my feet hanging over the edge. I swallow quickly, my stomach feeling queasy from the dizzying height. I sneak a look out of the corner of my eye. There's all types. Young guys, old ones, skinny, fat. Plain girls, pretty girls. Brown arms, white arms, arms with scars…

I know that scar.

No. It can't be.

I force myself to look at the face that goes with that scar. Her long, luscious hair floats in front of her as she leans over the edge. Staring downward.

They are all looking down. They always do. But my girl has her knees bent, and they're bouncing a little, as if she's ready to...

She jumps.

"No! Olivia! No!"

I push myself off that god-forsaken cliff. "Grab my hand! Olivia, grab my hand! Now!"

Finally, she lifts her face. Her eyes are wide open, and she looks peaceful, happy even. Then she sees me. "Jacob?" Confusion consumes her eyes. Fuck it all to hell. This never works. Nothing ever works.

"Everything's going to be okay," I lie. I push the air with my arms and try to propel myself toward her.

Our bodies crash into each other. I wrap my arms around her, and I hug her harder than I've ever hugged anyone in my life. "Hold on tight!" I say. She smells like Olivia. She feels like Olivia. I kiss her cheek. She tastes like Olivia.

Every time before when I've done this, I've kept my distance. I've held desperately onto hands, but I've always kept one free so I could fly. This time I don't, and it feels right. We're going to crash together, hit the ground together, die together. And I'm okay with that.

Only it doesn't happen. Just as we're about to cover the last few feet, I am ripped away by a force so sudden and so powerful that I'm left stunned. Even without my arms spread out like wings, I keep flying. I try to follow her down, but I can't. Some force field–like thing holds me back. And all I can do is watch in horror and disbelief as Olivia continues to fall and fall and fall until she slams into the ground.

Forty-Eight

JACOB

When I wake up, my neck is killing me. I turn on my side and nearly fall off the bed. I catch myself when my right hand hits carpet. Carpet? My new bedroom has hardwood floors, not carpet. Am I back at my dad's? I open my eyes and sit up. My truck? How am I in the truck? *Think!* Crap! Last night Olivia found the sketchbook. She stormed out. *Then what?* Right. I went to Nick's, had a beer. Then I went home. Only I didn't go home. I came here. Which is?

I look out the windshield. I'm in the parking lot of one of those 24-hour superstores. What town am I even in and how did I get here? The last thing I remember is a horrible headache, pulling off the road. But is this where I pulled off? I shake my head and pull my cellphone out of my pocket. Seven-thirty. *Shit!* School starts in a half hour. I rub the sleep out of my eyes, crank the engine, and tear out of the parking lot.

I feel nervous about something, but I don't know what. Is there a test today? Not that I would care. When have I cared about a test? Not since…Right. *Well, maybe it's about time you started caring, Jacob. You can't make excuses your whole life.*

I ask the GPS on my phone to find me the way to school. Fifty-seven minutes.

Damn it. Not only am I not going to be able to walk Olivia to school, I'm going to be late. *There's something else you're forgetting, Jacob. Something important.* What is it?

At a stoplight I pull up my contacts and tap on Olivia's name. She didn't even text me when I didn't show up this morning. Ouch.

I text her anyway, uneasiness spreading through my insides like honey.

As the miles fly by, I flash to the first day Olivia and I met, the first time I saw her scar. My stupid reaction because I felt like I'd seen that scar before.

I tap my fingers on the steering wheel and think. I think and I think and I try to force myself to remember, even though I can feel the edge of a headache creeping in. The light turns red, and I slam on my brakes. When the car stops, I close my eyes, clench my teeth. Force myself to keep thinking.

Come on, Jacob, you know this. Why?

A horn blares. My eyes fly open. Green light. I floor it.

Fuck it! It was that dream, that goddamn dream!

Did I see a scar that looked like hers in the crowd of people that is always hanging out by the cliff?

Makes sense. That's probably what's bothering me.

Only…

Think, Jacob, think!

Only, last night…

You're wrong, Jacob. And even if you're not, it doesn't mean anything.

Only, last night, I didn't just see a scar that looked like hers. I saw

Olivia.

She jumped.

And I couldn't save her.

Forty-Nine

OLIVIA

I wake up with a feeling of dread in my stomach. It takes me a minute to remember why, but the memory comes whooshing back pretty quick. Let's see. I ran out on Jacob because he was... that's right, drawing pictures of dead people. I might have overreacted a bit. And then I freaked out over Samantha's voice. I take a peek at my phone. Ten missed calls, all from Jacob. Just one text.

Please let me explain.

I sigh. Jacob has been awesome. Fun, kind, supportive. I need to listen to what he has to say, and tell him what he needs to know about me. Just not right now. Today is the zoology field trip—another thing I'm not exactly looking forward to. What if we have to look at birds? I can't stop thinking about birds. I see them everywhere, even where they aren't. I hear them singing, even in my sleep. When I fall asleep at night, they swoop and attack me. But worst of all are the ones that are saying my name. The last place I should be is anywhere birds could be. Maybe I should just stay home? I look in the mirror. That's a no-go.

161

As miserable as I feel, I look perfectly healthy. No way my mom is going to buy that I'm sick.

I step reluctantly into the shower, hoping the hot water will help me mellow out. No such luck. I get out of the shower as tense as when I went in. As I get ready to leave, I try to remember if we're supposed to bring a lunch or bring money for lunch. I don't know anymore. I grab a piece of leftover French bread wrapped in tinfoil and an apple, just in case, then I head out the door. I take my phone with me, but I power it down before I slip it into my pocket.

I know I should talk to Jacob. But I take the coward's way out and get in the Jeep, bypassing the corner with the dog where Jacob and I usually meet.

Fifty

JACOB

I keep driving to school, probably breaking all of the speeding laws, not caring. I call Olivia five times in a row, but she doesn't pick up. *Of course not, dummy, she's in class.* I send her a bunch more texts too, mostly at stoplights, but she doesn't answer those either. *That's because she's a good student, Jacob. And she's ignoring you because she thinks you're a sicko.*

I get to school near the end of first period. I sign in at the office and take my unexcused pass with me to English. *Take a deep breath. Get a grip. You'll see Olivia in second period.*

We're studying the Poe story about the heart under the floor. Is this woman crazy? Is she not aware that a girl from this school was murdered? And another in Essex? And...

"Jacob? Could you stop that tapping?" the teacher asks. "Or are you trying to set the scene for us?"

The class titters.

I put the pencil down and wipe the sweat off my forehead with my sleeve. Will it ever be second period?

As soon as the bell rings, I tear out of the room and bust my way down the hallway to chem class. I've never been happier to take in a long whiff of formaldehyde. I take my seat and tap a rhythm with two pencils on Olivia's desk as I wait for her to come in the room. But she never does, and when the bell rings, the room is only half full. A strange old woman is at Fredericks's desk. I get out of my seat and go up to one of the only girls left in the class. Charlotte, I think her name is.

"Where's Fredericks? And half the class?"

"Zoology field trip," she says. "He's one of the chaperones."

"That include Olivia?"

She smirks. "It's possible."

"Possible? How do I find out for sure?"

"I don't know. Text her?"

"I tried that. She's not answering."

"Yikes. Seems like you've been iced, Romeo."

The woman at the front of the room starts yelling at me to sit down.

"I don't feel well," I say. "Can I go to the nurse's office?"

She frowns at me. "Sit down."

I grip my stomach. "I think I'm going to throw up," I say, jogging toward her desk. I put one hand to my throat and clench my stomach muscles into a heaving motion.

"Go!" she shrieks seconds before I reach her.

Julia. If anyone would know where Olivia is, it would be Julia. I jog through the hallway, looking through the glass doors for her, until I see a random girl at a locker. "Julia Stevens. Do you know her?" I ask.

She pulls a trig book from her locker and looks up at me. "Uh, yeah?"

"Do you have her phone number?"

She shakes her head. "I don't think so."

"Or know what class she's in?"

She purses her lips. "Try choir."

"Thanks," I say, taking off. I stop and circle back. "Where would that be, by the way?"

"Second floor. Two eleven."

I rush the staircase, taking two at a time. Then I burst into the choir room in the middle of a Beatles song. Everyone turns to stare at me.

"Julia," I say, pausing to catch my breath. "Julia Stevens is needed in the office."

The choir teacher nods, and Julia raises her eyebrows but follows me out the door.

"What's going on?" she asks.

"Olivia. Do you know where she is?"

"She's on the field trip. The zoology one. Why?"

"She's not answering my texts."

Julia raises her eyebrows. "And that's why you called me out of class? A little clingy, don't you think? She probably can't hear anything over the drone of the bus. Wait, is something wrong?"

"It's just that she—I just—where's the field trip again?"

Julia tilts her head at me. "The Pittsburgh Zoo?"

"Right, okay, thanks." I start to back away. "Catch you later!"

"Hey, wait!" she says. "Give me your number, and I'll text you if I hear from her."

I come back, and we exchange phone numbers, then I take off down the hall and sprint down the stairs. This time I look for the nurse's office. By the time I get there, I'm coated in a sheen of sweat.

The nurse is taking the blood pressure of some gray-haired guy. I think it's one of the history teachers.

"Can I help you?" she asks.

"I'm burning up," I say. "Can you call my mom and tell her I need to go home?"

"Have you been running?" she asks.

165

"No, just sitting in class."

She releases the blood pressure cuff and grabs a thermometer from the medicine cabinet. "Here, put this under your tongue."

As she chats with the old guy, I turn my back on them and creep over to her desk, sticking the thermometer under the lamp for a few seconds.

"You do have a slight fever," she says. "If you want to dial your mom, I can talk to her."

After revealing my faux temperature to my mother, the nurse hands me the phone. "I'm on an interview," my mom says, her voice low. "Give me a few minutes to wrap it up and I'll be right there."

"It's okay. I can drive home. I've got the truck."

"Well…" I can hear the inner mom struggle in her voice. "If you're sure you don't mind. I'll come by to check on you at lunch."

"Don't bother. I'll probably be asleep." I slur my words, feeling like a jerk. "If I'm hungry, I'll find some soup."

"Hmm. Okay. Get better then. Call me if you need anything."

"I will," I say and hang up.

The nurse hands me a pass. "Be sure to sign out in the main office," she says.

I present my pass to the receptionist, looking and feeling suitably ill, even if it's not from a fever.

Once I'm in the parking lot, I pull up directions to the zoo on my phone. I tear out of the parking lot. *Slow down. The last thing you need is to get stopped.*

An hour later I'm at the zoo. I get out of the truck and slam the door. *Shit.* The zoo costs money. And I bet I don't have any. I pull out my wallet and check. Six dollars. *Damn it.* I'm pretty sure this is going to cost more than six dollars. I jerk open the door and climb back in the truck, searching the floor and seat cushions for coins. I come up with fifty-two cents. Planting my head on the steering wheel, I try to figure out what to do. *Wait a minute.* The card from my dad—it's in here somewhere…the glove compartment. What are the chances he sent some cash? As quick as I got my hopes up, I feel them deflate. Who would send cash? More importantly, who would send cash to their asshole kid who turned down a new Mustang?

I open the glove compartment and take out the envelope anyway. Sighing, I rip it open and slide the card out. As I open the card, I find a fifty staring back at me. Surely this is fake, because who would actually mail cash? I pick it up and inspect it. Looks real. *Well, hot damn. Thanks, Dad.* I force myself to read the card. Well, not the sappy verse, but the handwritten part. It says, *That old truck holds a lot of memories for me too.*

*How did he…*a lump forms at the back of my throat. *Way to take the high road, Dad.* I pull out my phone and send him a text.

Thanks for the card.

It hardly seems like enough, but it will have to do for now.

At the ticket counter I hand the cashier the fifty, half-expecting her to say she can't take anything larger than a twenty, but instead she gives me my change and a map. "Enjoy your visit," she says. I take off in a jog.

Shit! Two paths stretch before me. Which way to go? I head off toward the right, nearly taking out a toddler with a popsicle. Another kid seems to be pointing straight at me. "Look, Mommy, the tram! Please, can we take the tram? Please?"

I come to a dead stop and pivot toward where the kid is pointing. Meanwhile, the popsicle-kid mom rolls over my foot with her stroller.

Fifty-One

OLIVIA

A tram winds its way toward me, packed with excited toddlers, all waving. I wave back. A guy stands up, banging his head on the roof. "Olivia!" he shouts.

I squint. "Jacob?"

He looks like he's about to jump off. "Everyone please stay seated," calls the driver.

Jacob sits back down, his knees stuffed against the seat in front of him. "Meet me at the next stop?" he shouts, pointing ahead.

So much for turning off my phone. I look around to see if anyone from my class has noticed. "Okay."

I follow the tram to its stop and watch him get off, his hair shining in the sunlight. Despite my misgivings, my heart feels lighter just looking at him.

"What are you doing here?" I ask when he reaches me.

"I didn't want to miss out on a good field trip," he says, but his voice is lacking its usual lighthearted tone. "It's good to see you," Jacob says, giving me a hug like he hasn't seen me in days.

"It hasn't even been twenty-four hours."

"I know," he says, "but when you didn't answer my texts…"

"I turned my phone off. Sorry. Does Mr. Cushing know you're here?"

He shakes his head. "No, and I'd like to keep it that way, if I can."

"Right."

He takes my hand tentatively, no doubt afraid I'll shake it away. It sends a good type of chill up my arm.

"If I promise not to talk about last night, can I walk with you?"

I nod. "Sure."

"So what's there to see?"

"We're supposed to be observing the animals and taking notes," I say. "The monkeys are that way. I haven't been there yet."

"Lead the way," Jacob says.

We walk slowly, hand in hand, the rush of the crowd funneling around us, until we reach the monkey exhibit.

"Why don't we sit on this bench and you can take your notes?" says Jacob.

We sit on the bench, and I take out my notebook, not really sure what I should be writing. A baby monkey seems to be playing with something resembling an acorn while his mother grooms him. Clutching his acorn, the monkey hops onto a tree stump. Then he drops his acorn and hops back down again, searching for it in the long grasses. He finally locates it, then scampers off.

"You're even more pretty when you smile." Jacob runs his finger along my neck. "Am I forgiven yet?"

I turn my face toward his, but before I can say anything, he places his fingers gently over my mouth. "Nah, don't answer that yet." He sighs, and his eyes look troubled. "We have to talk first. Want to get some lunch?"

"I have a bit of bread and an apple in my bag, but somehow I don't think that's going to fill you up."

"You're probably right. How about I grab something from the snack bar first?"

"Sure." I let Jacob take my hand again, and we walk in silence to the snack bar.

"I'll stake out a table."

"Don't bother," Jacob says, pulling me into the line with him. "There's plenty of tables. Besides, I bet you wouldn't turn down some lemonade in a souvenir cup. My treat."

"Shelling out the big bucks, aren't we? Must be a pretty serious conversation."

Jacob gives a half-smile but doesn't answer. At the counter he orders a burger and fries and two lemonades. When our food is ready, we head to a table in the shade.

"I'm just going to go wash my hands in the bathroom," I say. "Back in a minute."

"Aren't there any hand-sanitizing stations out here?" he asks.

I look around. "Nope, don't see any. Do you?"

"I guess not." Jacob seems unduly disappointed. "I guess I should wash up too. Meet you right back here."

Fifty-Two

JACOB

As I head into the bathroom, I realize that it's been a while since I've gone. I do my business, then wash my hands, feeling ridiculous for not wanting to let Olivia out of my sight when she said she wanted to use the bathroom. It was stupid of me to rush here in a panic on account of some crazy dreams. Just exactly why was I so freaked out anyhow?

I'm waving my hands under the hand dryer when I hear a scream. I break out in a cold sweat. *Olivia!*

I burst through the bathroom door and locate the table where I left my burger and fries. Olivia's not there. My heart is pounding. I whip my head around right and left. No Olivia. Is she still in the bathroom? Did someone grab her in there? Should I check? A young girl walks calmly out of the women's room. "Is everything okay in there?" I shout at her. She looks at me as if I'm a madman, hugging the wall to stay as far away from me as possible. Another woman, probably her mom, pulls her off to the side and shoots me a dirty look. Where is Olivia?

Doesn't anyone else care? I snake my way through the other tables, desperate to find her.

I round a corner. A girl with a purple backpack, her back to me, is rubbing her raven-black hair.

"Olivia?"

She turns around. "Oh, hey," she says.

"What happened? Was that you who screamed?"

"Yeah, that was me." She looks sheepish. "Please don't tell me you heard that all the way in the bathroom."

"Not exactly," I lie. "What happened? What's wrong?"

"It's just…" She hesitates, as if she's not sure she should tell me.

"It's just what? Tell me."

"It's just there was this bird, and I…I thought…well, it looked kind of interesting, so I was following it and then…"

"Then what?"

"And then it pecked me on the head. I think."

"It pecked you on the head? Here, let me see. Where did it peck you?"

"Right here," she says, pointing.

I run my fingers through her hair, pushing it aside to get to the scalp. "Hmm, I don't see anything, so it looks like it didn't break the skin at least. That's good, right?"

"I guess so," she says, sounding uncertain.

"You don't think it could have rabies, do you?"

"No, I'm pretty sure only mammals can get rabies."

"Oh, right. But here, I'll check my phone just to be sure." I pull out my phone and quickly type the question. "Yep, you're right. Obviously you learned at least one thing in that zoology class."

"At least there's that," she says. "Come on, let's go eat."

Back at our table, our food is undisturbed. We sit down, and Olivia pulls out her bread and apple.

"Fries?" I ask, pushing my plate toward her.

"Not now, thanks," she says and takes a bite from her apple.

I spread mustard on my burger and take a few bites, trying to figure out what I'm going to say.

"Look. I know you were upset about the drawings you saw. And I know that drawing dead girls is definitely not cool. It's just that sometimes when I'm worrying about things, it helps to draw. Even when what comes out is just plain weird. So I'm sorry about that. But there's actually something else I wanted to talk to you about too."

She pushes her hair out of her eyes and wipes her lips with a napkin. "I'm listening," she says.

"I've been having these dreams." I open a salt packet and try to sprinkle the contents lightly on my fries. I end up pouring the entire packet out in one spot. "Ever since I was in that car accident with my friend Ricky."

I glance at Olivia. She's squinting at me, her brow furrowed. I take a deep breath and try to spread the salt around. "The dream always starts the same. I'm standing at the edge of this enormous cliff. It's more like the Grand Canyon, actually. And there are all these other people lined up along the edge. Every time I have the dream, someone jumps. Afterward I can't always remember what the people looked like, but sometimes I remember pieces."

She's looking at me as if she doesn't get it. "Okay."

"Your friend Samantha, when I first saw her picture, I felt like I had seen her before, like maybe in that dream. And then that other girl who was killed, on the news she was wearing a dolphin shirt, and there was this girl in my dream with a dolphin necklace. So these dreams, it almost feels like they were…"

"Premonitions?"

I nod. "I know, it sounds crazy, even to me."

"Dreams can be weird."

I open another salt packet. Make another mess. "The reason why I had to come here today, why I needed to see you, why I didn't even want to let you go to the bathroom? It's because last night I had the same dream. And the girl who jumped...was you."

Olivia puts down her apple. "So you're saying what, exactly? That I'm going to be the Sweet Dreams Strangler's next victim?"

"When you say it like that, it does sound pretty lame." I pick up a fry and try to shake the salt off it. "I'm sorry. I don't know why I let a stupid dream get me so worked up. I shouldn't have said anything to you. I mean, look, here you are, you're fine." I shake my head as I figure it out. "We were fighting last night, so it makes sense that I would dream about you. And then in the dream, when I couldn't hold on to you, well, I guess that was because I was worried about losing you."

She puts her hand on mine. "Don't be sorry. If I wouldn't have overreacted about the drawings, you wouldn't have had the dream."

I turn my hand over and play with her fingers. "We good then?"

She smiles. "Yeah. We're good."

I finish my burger, and Olivia finishes her apple, but she doesn't touch her bread. At least she drinks the lemonade. Half the fries are so covered in salt that I can't eat them.

"Don't you want something else to eat?" I ask. "You barely had anything."

"I'm not that hungry."

"You want to see the rest of the animals then?"

"Actually, I'm super tired. I could use a nap. Let's find a bench where we won't see anyone from school."

"No problem."

Olivia gets up and throws out her trash. All except for the souvenir cup. We find a bench in a place out of the way. I sit, and Olivia rests her head on my lap.

"You know what?" I ask a minute later.

Olivia doesn't answer. As I look down at her, I realize that she's not ignoring me. She's asleep.

After a half-hour, I wake her up. "What time does your bus leave?"

"Two o'clock. What time is it?" She sits up quickly.

"It's one o'clock. You've been asleep for a half-hour."

"Yeah, sorry. I guess I didn't get enough sleep last night."

"Right. But you've been tired all the time lately. You really need to see a doctor."

"Which is it, the Sweet Dreams Strangler or cancer?"

"Huh?"

"Your dream. The one that told you I'm going to die."

"I thought we agreed that was just..."

"Kidding. Get over yourself already." She sits up, looking ready to conquer the world. "Now let's go see ourselves some giraffes."

"You got it," I say.

In the hour we have left, we see the giraffes and the zebras and every type of bear. At the hippos, Olivia leans over the barrier. The hair cascading over her face doesn't hide her smile. "I love how chubby these guys are."

"Are you saying you'd like me better if I gained a few pounds?"

She turns to me and taps her index finger against my chest. "No, Jacob, I like you just the way you are." She takes a step closer. "Crazy dreams and all," she whispers.

I push the hair away from her face with my palms and brush my lips against hers. Her lips answer mine, and it's not until a wagon hits me in the back of the knees, making me stumble forward, that we break apart.

"If you were done, you could have just said so," she says, laughing as we catch our balance. "I've got to get on the bus."

I tuck her head under my chin and hold her close. "Ride home with me instead."

"Right. Because Mr. Cushing will really go for that."

"Can I at least see you tonight?"

"I guess so. Come by after dinner." She slides her fingertips up my arms. "But right now I better get on that bus."

"Got it." We walk out of the zoo, my arm around her waist. If anyone from school notices us, they don't say anything.

When the bus is in sight, Olivia stops, then pulls my neck down and plants a quick kiss on my lips. "You better stay here because I don't want to know what Mr. Cushing will do if he sees you." She takes a step and then stops and looks back at me. "On second thought, that might be kind of funny. For me, that is. Definitely not for you."

"Go on, you." I give her a gentle push. Staying far away from the bus, I make my way to my truck and get in, turning the key just long enough to put the windows down. I listen to the country music play until the power cuts out. Then I sit and watch the bus until everyone has gotten on and it pulls away.

Time to get out of here. I put my foot on the brake and crank the ignition. I'm just sliding the gearshift into reverse when my phone rings. I glance at the screen. *Shit.* It's my mom. I'm guessing she found out about my unauthorized field trip. Only one way to be sure.

"Hi, Mom."

"We got him, Jacob."

"Excuse me, what?" I kill the engine.

"We caught the Sweet Dreams Strangler."

"That...that's great," I say, stunned.

"It is," she says, not sounding as relieved as she should. "You want to know how, Jacob?"

"Um, yeah, sure."

"I told my team I thought we should interview James Callaghan again. He was one of our original suspects who seemed to have a rock-solid alibi for the fourth girl's murder. For Samantha's murder. When we got to the guy's house in Pine Grove, he was pulling out of the driveway, so we followed him."

Pine Grove. That's the city where I was last night. Correction. Where I fell asleep in a parking lot...

"Are you listening to me, Jacob?"

"Yeah, of course I am."

"We follow him to the middle of nowhere until the guy figures out that we're onto him and leads us on a high-speed chase. When we finally catch him, guess what we find in the car?"

"I don't know. What?"

"We find his middle-aged sister in the trunk. Dead. Turns out he blamed her for not calling the cops when their stepdad beat him as a kid and she was a teenager. So he's been killing teenage girls who he thinks aren't paying enough attention to their siblings. The guy confessed to everything except for Samantha's murder."

"Why would he have confessed to everything except that?"

"I don't know. All I know is..."

"What?"

"That you've got a lot of explaining to do," my mom says, her voice strained. "How did you know?" she hisses. She continues without waiting for me to respond. "My boss wanted to know why I suspected Callaghan."

"I don't get it. What do I have to do with this?"

"It was the drawing you put in my file, Jacob."

"What drawing? What are you talking about?" Okay, sure, I was going through my mom's file yesterday. What did she expect, leaving it out where anyone could find it? But it's not like I would add anything to her file. I'm not that stupid. Unless when I was scooping all the papers back up...

"You mean the woman? The sketch of the woman?"

"What other sketch did you put in there?" She sounds like she's about to lose it.

"None. I didn't even mean to stick that one in there. I just…"

"It took me a while to figure it out, but her face looked familiar. I felt like I had seen that woman before, but I didn't know where," my mom says. "And then it hit me. She was the one who answered the door when we went to interview Callaghan. The picture you drew, that was Callaghan's sister. My boss saw the picture, Jacob. There's going to be questions, lots of them. I need you to come right home."

"Okay, right. I'm on my way." The line goes dead. I close my eyes, suddenly nauseous.

This is good news, right? They caught the Sweet Dreams Strangler. What does it matter how they figured it out? Or that he didn't confess to Samantha's murder yet?

The important thing is that there's no more danger. Olivia's safe.

Unless…

Unless I'm the one she should be afraid of.

Fifty-Three

OLIVIA

Back at home, in my sanctuary on the third floor, I fling open the doors, close my eyes, and stretch my arms like wings at my sides out on the balcony where Jacob and I danced for the first time. The wind blows hair in my face, tickling my cheek, reminding me of Jacob's touch. The buzz of the neighbor's lawn mower distracts a bit from the memory, so I hum a Thomas Rhett song to block it out.

At the zoo I was all over the map, emotion-wise. Cold and then hot, cool, warm, hot again. Jacob's dream made him worry that I would die, but the ironic thing is that I don't have to die for him to lose me. I just have to tell him the truth.

When (if) I tell Jacob my secret, he will know just how crazy I am. There will be no taking it back. He will either take off running and lose me quickly or stay close by as I fade away. As I am examined and medicated and watched. There will be no more balconies (she could jump), no more dances (I'm not sure she should leave the house), just the buzz of a lawn mower muted through a tightly locked window.

179

It won't be much longer now. Like crazy father, like crazy daughter. I know because of what that bird whispered to me today right before he pecked my head.

That bird, he whispered,

You're next.

Fifty-Four

JACOB

When I get home, there's a dark-haired man in a suit hovering over our kitchen table. "Sit down, Jacob," my mom says. "This is my boss, Aaron Weaver. He has some questions we need answered." My mom's face is pinched, and her heels click on the tile as she paces back and forth.

"How do you know this man, Jacob?" Boss-man slaps a photo on the table.

"Is he the Sweet Dreams Strangler?"

"You tell me."

"I don't know him. I've never seen him before."

"Where were you last night? Your mom said you weren't here."

Why would my mom tell this guy where I was or wasn't last night? "I stayed over at a friend's house. I was at Nick's. I texted her." God, I hope Nick will back me up. The last thing I want to tell this guy is that I spent the night in a parking lot. In Pine Grove.

"And this morning?"

"I was at school."

"The whole day?"

"I…I went home sick."

"What time was that?"

"Second period. Nine o'clock."

"It's obvious you didn't come home. Where'd you go?"

"Um, the zoo?"

"What were you doing at the zoo?"

"It was for a field trip."

"First you said you were sick. Now you say you went on a field trip. Which was it?" Another slap on the table. My mom's lifting up her hair, twisting it into a bun. Click, click, click go the heels.

"I wasn't supposed to be on the field trip. It wasn't for my class. But my girlfriend was on the trip, so I pretended to be sick and drove to the zoo instead."

"What time did you get there?"

"About ten, ten-fifteen."

"Who saw you there?"

"My girlfriend."

"Anyone else?"

"The workers, I guess. The ticket lady. Maybe someone from the class. You can check the GPS on my phone. Can't it tell you where I've been?"

"You could have given it to your girlfriend."

"The bus left over an hour before I did. Besides, if I had something to do with this creep, why would I lead my mom to him?"

"Guilty conscience. You wanted to get caught."

What a fucking jerk. "My mom said you caught the guy. So what did he say when you asked him about an accomplice? Did he mention me? Huh?"

Weaver's confidence flickers.

"No, of course he didn't," I shout. "Because I never met the man. And I didn't have anything to do with these murders."

"Where were you the night Courtney Walker died, Jacob?" My mom's boss eyes me suspiciously, an edge to his voice. I slouch in my chair. Finding a leftover blueberry bagel, I poke my finger through the center and swirl it around.

"I was home." And then I went for a ride. And I got a headache. Pulled over. Fell asleep. Woke up in Essex, the town where the girl was killed. Shit. This looks bad. This feels bad. And I'm lying to the FBI. What if this guy is right to suspect me? Had I seen that girl? Had something to do with her death?

Impossible. Crazy. Or was it? I had no choice but to lie.

"The whole evening?"

"Yeah, sure," I say with the best teenage jerk-face bluster I can manage. Casual and annoying.

The boss-man snatches the bagel away from me and slams it onto the table.

Would they find my tire tracks near the scene of the murder? Had I been close? I don't even know. All I know is that if they do find that clue, I'm toast. Game over.

"How about the week before, when Samantha Young died, just days after you moved here? Where were you then? Were you with James Callaghan? Were you his apprentice?"

"I told you I don't know Callaghan. I've never met him."

"So why did you draw this picture of his sister?" He slaps my drawing of the woman down in front of me.

"I don't know. I just drew that face. I didn't mean for it to look like anyone. It probably just reminded my mom of this guy's sister. Doesn't mean they're the same person."

He smacks a photo down next to my drawing. "It doesn't, huh?"

I convince myself that there's only a minimal resemblance between the two images. That red shirt, the one the woman in the photo is wearing, seems familiar, but then a lot of things seem that way lately, courtesy no doubt of my head making contact with a dashboard.

"Maybe this guy threatened you. Threatened your mom. We've got him now. There's no reason for you to hold back. We can put you and your mom in protective custody if he told you he has someone on the outside."

"I told you. I don't know anything about the guy who did this."

Boss-man shakes his head. My mom puts her arm on his shoulder. "Aaron, can I talk to you?"

Boss-man shakes his head again and gets up. He follows her into the bedroom. They shut the door, but it doesn't keep me from following them or putting my eye in the crack of the door.

"I don't know how long I can keep this quiet. I should really bring him in. You know that."

"Aaron, he's my son. I know him." She takes his hands.

"Do you really? How long has it been?" He puts his hand on her face.

Shit. Aaron is the guy I saw sneaking out of our house that morning. Which explains why he conducted his interview at our kitchen table instead of at the FBI field office. But this is never going to work. This guy is never going to accept that the resemblance between the two images is just a coincidence. It's not in his nature.

I barge into the bedroom. "Does the FBI know you've been sleeping with my mom?"

"Jacob!" says my mom.

A vein bulges in Aaron's face. Mission accomplished. *Sorry, Mom.* I've put him on the defensive, if only for a few seconds.

"I guess that's a no," I say. "Well, I guess everyone lies. I mean, in the case of you and my mom, it's not exactly a lie, is it? Just something you conveniently haven't mentioned at the office. Yet. I'm sure you haven't mentioned it because you're trying to protect her. The same way I didn't mention the real reason I suspected Callaghan."

All the color in my mom's face drains, and Aaron looks ready to slap a pair of cuffs on me.

I scramble to make up some bullshit that will be easier for this guy to believe than the truth. "Don't worry. I didn't lie about knowing Callaghan. What I didn't tell you is that I've spent a lot of time going through my mom's files. The ones she's always leaving out where anyone can find them."

Aaron's eyes shift to my mom, who looks uncomfortable. She knows she hasn't been good about putting things away. I plow ahead. "I guess I read too many mystery novels when I was younger because I always fancied myself a bit of a detective. That and my girlfriend was close to one of the victims, Samantha, so I wanted to help her friend get justice, as they say." I shrug my shoulders, then pick up a string of beads from my mom's dresser and rotate it from hand to hand.

"When Mom was asleep, I'd go through the files and try to figure it out myself. Mom always had Callaghan's file on top, so I figured she saw him as the most likely suspect. Maybe that's why I latched onto him too." I play more with the beads, trying to think. *Come on Jacob, you can do this.*

"The file mentioned an abusive past. That plus the fact that he was living with his sister got me wondering if his killing all of those girls was a way of getting back at his sister for not doing something about it. And if so, sooner or later he was going to kill her too."

My mom grabs my left hand, stopping me from transferring the beads. She holds on tightly, her nails digging into my skin ever so slightly. I open my palm and hand her the beads, refusing to look her in the eye. "So I made a sketch of the sister and left it in the file. I'm sure my mom knew all of this subconsciously. My sketch just gave her a nudge in the right direction."

When I finish my speech, Aaron claps. Only his clapping doesn't sound very sincere. "Just one problem with your revised account of events," he says.

"Yeah? What's that?"

"It doesn't explain Callaghan's denying responsibility for Samantha's murder. You know, she's the one your girlfriend was so close to? He admits to all of the other murders, but not that one."

I shrug, palms up. "You know, that does sound like a bit of a challenge. But I guess that's why you're in the FBI and not me."

Fifty-Five

OLIVIA

acob comes over after dinner. He tells a few jokes to my mom, then he casually takes my hand and we slip away to the third floor. He sprawls sideways on the couch, his legs in front of him and taps his lap. "Sit."

"I'm too heavy."

"Nah, you're just right." He tugs my arm until I'm on his lap, resting my head on his chest, my legs between his legs. Then he wraps his arms around me. "They found the Sweet Dreams Strangler."

"I heard."

"The guy killed his own sister. My mom went to interview the guy again because of some picture I drew of a woman that kind of looked like her. Weird, huh?"

I twist around to look at him. "What? Do you think it had something to do with…"

"Nah. I'm with you on that now. I mean, we all see what we want to see, don't we? My mom sees a picture that kind of looks like someone she's seen before. She fills in the blanks, but only because she's got good reasons to suspect the guy in the first place. End of story."

I relax back against him, and he holds me tighter. "So how about I drive you to the doctor tomorrow?" he says.

"Tomorrow's Saturday. Besides, I'm babysitting."

"Monday then?"

"Okay."

"Okay? You mean it?" Jacob squeezes my hand.

I squeeze back. "Yeah. I promise."

"Do we get to skip school?"

"Only if they can't fit me in after school."

He sighs. "Why do you have to be so responsible?"

"I'm not always responsible."

"Ha. Prove it."

"How?"

"Hmm." He appears to be stumped. "Aha! Got it! Let me stay over. I can pretend to leave and then hide in the closet again so your mom doesn't know." He kisses the top of my head.

"I don't know, Jacob."

"We don't have to do anything. Just let me spend the night next to you." He runs his hand through my hair. "You don't have to answer yet. Just think about it."

"Just think about it, huh?" I turn over so I'm facing him and kiss his lips.

"Uh-huh."

I kiss his neck, and then I slide his shirt up and my lips move across his chest. His shirt comes off and so does mine, and I'm glad I have on the bra that I do even though I don't think I'll be wearing it much longer. Jacob slides one of my straps down and then the other, and I enjoy the look on his face as he admires the view. His hands reach around back and fumble a bit with the clasp. We both laugh for just a moment, but then he works it free and takes it off, and he's kissing me there and it feels so good I never want this to stop.

After a few minutes, his hands slide across my jeans, and it's as if I'm floating.

"I love you," Jacob whispers, and I want to believe that he means forever, no matter what, even when he knows the truth, even though I know it's not fair.

I love you too, my heart whispers, only I don't say it out loud.

I lie on top of Jacob and listen to the beating of his heart. My hands move downward. I run my fingers along his legs and watch a smile drift slowly across his face. But then he gently takes my hands and brings them to his chest. "It's not that I don't want to, but isn't your mom downstairs?"

"Now who's the responsible one?"

"You still haven't given me an answer about my hiding in the closet. I can do stealth quite well, in case you didn't know." He kisses my neck.

"Oh, I'm sure you can. It's just…"

"Don't worry about it. Tonight's probably not the best night for me to be out all night anyway. My mom's not my biggest fan right now. And she may have started reading some parenting books because she used the word 'curfew' as I was walking out the door."

"Why? What happened?"

Jacob's brow furrows. "Let's just say I didn't make the best first impression on her boyfriend. Who also happens to be her boss."

"Her boss? Is that allowed?"

He shrugs. "Beats the hell out of me."

"So what's he like?"

"A total…" Jacob stops himself and takes a deep breath. "He'll take some getting used to. But I think he means well." Jacob brushes his hand along my stomach. "But enough about that guy. The least I could do is help you put this back on before I go." He grabs my bra and swings it in the air.

"Give me that!" I try to grab it from him, but he's determined, so I let him.

Jacob leaves with barely enough time to get home before his curfew. "No speeding," I say.

"Of course not. If I get home too early, my mom will ask what we did." He grins. "And then I'll have to lie. On the other hand, if I get home just late enough for her to yell at me, she'll probably forget to ask."

"You have an answer for everything, don't you?"

"Actually not." Jacob sighs and then runs his hands through my hair and kisses me softly and gently. It's the kind of kiss that makes me think of butterflies dancing in the air.

Fifty-Six

JACOB

⁓◦⧼∾◦⧽◦⁓

I don't know if it's because he has a nagging doubt that I have some sort of relationship to the Sweet Dreams Strangler, or because he's decided that now that the cat's out of the bag he can stop sneaking around, but Aaron never goes home. When I come down for breakfast, there he is, hanging out in the kitchen as if he belongs. Barefoot. Shirtless. Wearing a pair of pajama bottoms that I doubt he had stashed in his briefcase. Lazily buttering a piece of toast. I want to take the butter dish and shove it right in his face, but instead I take a deep breath and try to chill.

"Morning, Jacob," he says, as if this is the most normal thing in the world. I want him to fumble over the coffee pot, proving that he doesn't know jack shit about this place or my mom, that he was only here once or twice, that he doesn't belong. But he reaches into the cupboard where we keep the mugs and takes down my mom's favorite, the one she bought at Hershey Park years ago, during my brother's first and only trip to an amusement park, and reaches for a second.

"Coffee?" he asks, looking over his shoulder at me.

"No, thanks," I say, and I watch him find the coffee grounds and filters in the first place he looks. I realize that my mom's life has gone on without me or my dad in it. I grab an apple from the refrigerator, run it under the kitchen faucet, and then, straddling a chair at the table, I take a bite.

"Your mom and I are going to take a ride to the cider mill for some cider and doughnuts this afternoon. You want to come along?"

"What, it's Saturday and you guys aren't going in to the office?"

"We caught the bad guy, as they say. In this business, you learn to take a breather when you can."

"I'm sure you do. It's not my thing, but thanks anyway." I'm expecting the words to come out biting and sarcastic, and probably he does too, but somehow they don't. "I've got time for a quick game of basketball though."

I'm not sure if I meant that as a test, and if I did, what the correct answer was supposed to be, but either way, he tilts his head and quietly says, "You're on." Then he takes a final bite of toast and leaves the room. I watch the coffee drip into the pot for a few moments before I get up and go to my room to change.

When I get back to the kitchen, Aaron is there, this time wearing gym shorts and a T-shirt that he must also keep here, along with a pair of running shoes. Do he and my mom run together, or did they used to before I moved in? He pours coffee into the two mugs, takes a drink from one, and pours cream into the other one.

"I'll take it to her," I say.

Aaron nods and hands me the mug. "See you outside."

I walk down the hallway, only partially succeeding at not spilling the coffee down my hand. I switch the mug to my other hand and shake off the scalding liquid before it stings too badly, then dry my hand on my shorts. When I get to my mom's room, I knock.

"Come in," she says. I open the door, thinking she's probably expecting it to be Aaron, hoping she's wearing clothes.

She is. "Oh, Jacob." She's standing in front of the mirror putting on earrings. I hand her the mug.

"Thanks." She smiles.

"Your boyfriend agreed to play basketball with me," I say.

"Go easy on him, will you?"

"Yeah, I'm thinking that since Aaron is an FBI agent, it's me who needs to be worried."

She winces. "You might be right about that," she says, laughing just a little. Her face sobers quickly. "Jacob, there was no photo of Callaghan's sister in that file. So how is it that you drew her?"

Fuck it. Now what do I say? She jumped off a cliff in a dream I had? That's a no-go. Any resemblance my drawing has to that guy's sister is just a coincidence anyway, isn't it? How could it be anything else?

Think!

I finally come up with an answer I think she'll believe. "You know how quickly you can pull up a picture of someone on the Internet? Even serial killers use Facebook."

My mom's brow furrows, but she nods. "We'll talk later," she says, and leaves the room

I collapse on the bed and try to pull myself back together. *Close one, genius.*

The basketball game with Aaron is equal parts sweaty and vicious, and what Aaron lacks in technical skill he makes up in body checking. I beat him by six points, falling to the ground as I let loose the final basket. Aaron reaches down to pull me up. "Not bad, kid," he says and wipes the sweat dripping off his forehead. My mom is off to the side, hands wrapped around her coffee mug, voice raw after cheering for both sides. As I look at her, the sun beats into my eyes, and I blink. They feel a bit wet, but I'm not sure if it's the sun or the glimpse I've just had into an alternate reality, the one in which my dad and brother are standing here beside me.

Fifty-Seven

JACOB

Wⁱᵗ my mom and Aaron are at the cider mill, I video chat with Olivia.

"I'm glad you were here last night." Her lips curve into a small smile. So beautiful.

"Me too." I smile back. "When can I see you?"

She laughs, and it reminds me of the wind chimes outside my dad's house. "I can see something in your eyes, and I'm not getting the homework vibe from it."

"You're right. It's called lust."

She laughs again. "I'm leaving now to babysit Owen. I should be back by four. Meet me at my place? We can go out." She blushes. "Or maybe stay in."

"Now whose eyes are spilling secrets?" *I need a cold shower.*

We say goodbye, and I take that shower. Then I slap on a pair of jeans and a shirt, settle on the couch, and flip on the TV. I try to watch a sitcom, but I can't stop thinking of Olivia's face, her smile. Her scar. How could her dad do that to her? I turn off the TV and toss the remote on the coffee table, then I grab my laptop out of my room.

I only read one article about the fire, but it's enough to forever sear the details in my mind.

Olivia, seven years old, sleeping in an abandoned farmhouse. Abandoned because of another little girl who died in the same house.

Olivia's father buying the accelerant in town that same day, just hours before he used it.

An all-consuming fire.

Olivia trying desperately to get back into the house she just escaped, screaming *Daddy...*

Fifty-Eight

OLIVIA

───⌘───

As soon as Owen's parents are out the door, Owen wants me to push him on the swing in the backyard. "Please, Olivia. P-lease! I'll share my slime with you!"

"Tell you what. I'll push you as long as you promise I don't have to play with slime when we come back in."

That was obviously the wrong thing to say. Owen looks like he's going to cry.

"Kidding!" I say, not meaning it. "Swing first, and then slime. I even have a new slime recipe for you to try out."

"Is it green?" He bounces excitedly.

"It's whatever color your mom's laundry detergent is."

"Oh." He sounds dejected. "It's blue."

"Blue is an awesome color!"

He gives me the you've-got-to-be-kidding look.

"Okay, well, we'll find something better on the Internet."

"Promise?"

"Definitely."

We high-five.

Owen rushes out the sliding glass door to the swing set. "Push me, Olivia! Push me!"

Now that, I can handle. I give him a big push. He points his toes toward the sky and flings his head back. If only life were that simple at seventeen.

I slide into the swing next to him, push off, and try it myself. I'm leaning back, soaking in the sun and the sky, getting lost in just being.

"Hey!" shouts Owen. "You stopped pushing!"

So much for getting lost in the moment. I jump off my swing and reposition myself behind Owen. "Pump your legs, buddy. You go higher."

He pumps, and he's going up and up, so high that there's a catch at the highest point.

I give him eight or nine good pushes, and then he jumps off and runs to the trees at the edge of the property.

"It's back!" Owen yells. He bends down, like he's petting something. Oh, crap. He's petting the wildlife. He's going to get bit! What *is* that?

"Wait, Owen, don't touch!" I run up behind him.

"It's okay. It's a toy bird. It's remote control. Just watch."

Sure enough, the little bird starts flying into the woods.

Bird. Another fricking bird. Hey, but at least Owen sees it too. That part's not my imagination.

Olivia!

Sure enough, this one is calling my name too.

Olivia!

Samantha's voice, and it sounds frantic. Samantha was Owen's babysitter. Could she have programmed her voice on this toy? She could have—but there would have been no reason for her to program it to say my name. Great.

Damn it! While I've been standing here in a stupor, Owen's been running after the bird. Maybe it's one of those drone things. Kind of cool, I suppose, but I have no desire to get lost in the woods with Owen. Not to mention the fact that Samantha's voice is sounding more and more shrill. It's starting to make me feel sick.

"Owen! Owen, come back here right now!" I can't see Owen anymore, but I hear the crunch of sticks up ahead where he must be. My heart is thumping, and the sweat on my neck turns all prickly and cold. I don't like this. I don't like this at all. "Owen!" I run after him. A twig scrapes my face, and a vine trips me and then clings to my leg as I keep running.

I see a flash of red up ahead. Owen's shirt. Thank God. At least he's stopped. "Owen! Stay right there! Don't move!"

I finally reach him and put my arm on his shoulder. We're in a clearing next to the river.

"Look, Olivia!" He's pointing over the river, where that damn bird is hovering. There's a small boat tied up along the shore. It must belong to the guy flying this thing. Owen's leaning toward the water as he points, way too close to the edge. Dirt crumbles by his feet. I grab him around the waist and pull him back. At the same time, someone grabs me from behind, pulling us both back from the edge. We fall backward into the dirt, but at least not into the water.

Relieved, I turn my head, wanting to thank our drone-flying hero, but before I can get any words out, a cloth is pressed tightly against my nose and mouth. I try to scream, but it comes out as a muffled squeak. The last sensation I have is of someone pulling off my shoes.

Fifty-Nine

JACOB

I show up on Olivia's doorstep right at four. I ring the bell, but no one's there, so I sit on the porch step to wait. I text Olivia, but she doesn't answer. I guess she's either doing her job or driving.

I'm still sitting on the steps, playing a mind-numbing game on my phone, when Olivia's mom pulls into the driveway. "Hi, Jacob! Mind giving me a hand with these groceries?"

"Sure thing." I pop up and cross the small strip of grass to the driveway. "Paper bags. Old school." I scoop a couple into each arm.

"I use them for the recycling. Olivia's not back yet?"

"Nope."

Olivia's mom sighs. "People have so little respect for their babysitters. Would it kill them to get back when they say they're going to?"

"I know, right?"

We climb the porch steps and lug the grocery bags into the kitchen. "I'll go grab the rest."

"Thanks, Jacob." Olivia's mom starts unloading the bags onto the counter.

As I head back outside, I check my phone again. Nothing from Olivia. It's been thirty minutes. The uncomfortable feeling that's been souring my stomach since I first sat on the porch steps starts kicking into high gear.

"Olivia have any idea when she'll be back?" her mom asks as I set the last few bags on the counter.

"Actually, she hasn't gotten back to me yet."

"Hmm. Let me try calling." Her mom closes the refrigerator and dials. "Nothing. Well, I don't know what to tell you, Jacob. Maybe she's giving the boy a bath?"

"Isn't it a bit early for that?"

"Not if he was off playing in the mud."

"I guess." *Or maybe she's fallen asleep? That doctor's appointment on Monday can't come soon enough.*

"Jacob, would you mind going over there to check? I'm sure everything is fine, but I'd feel better knowing for sure."

"Of course. I was thinking the same thing."

"You'll have her text me?"

"Will do."

When I get to Owen's house, I ring the bell, fairly certain that Owen will outrun Olivia to the door. But when I ring it a second time, it's the only sound I hear echoing through the house. I jog around to the backyard. *Of course they wouldn't be inside on a day like today.* On my way, I scoop up a football from the edge of the driveway and prepare to launch it at Owen. "Heads up!" I shout, my eyes sweeping the area for Owen's blond hair. Finding neither Owen nor Olivia, I drop the football and run up to the sliding glass door at the back of the house, my heart pounding, but not from the exercise. I cup my hands around my eyes and press against the glass, trying to see in. I test the door. It's unlocked. I slide it open just a bit and stick my head in. "Olivia?

Owen?"

Should I go inside? Maybe they're both napping. Owen mentioned something about a nap the last time I was here. As I'm standing there debating, a car pulls into the driveway, and a couple gets out.

Great. This isn't going to look weird at all. I step away from the door and make my way to the driveway.

"Can we help you with something?" asks the woman, shading her eyes with her hand.

"You must be Owen's parents. I'm Olivia's...boyfriend, Jacob. She was late coming back, so I was just checking..."

"Oh, hi, Jacob. Nice to meet you. I'm Sharon, and this is my husband, Dave." A burly guy in a Penn State T-shirt nods at me. Good thing he didn't find me inside his house. "Sorry we're late. I hope Olivia saw my text. Are they in the backyard?"

"Uh no, actually not. And they weren't answering the door. Maybe they're at the park?"

"Probably," says Sharon. "Come on in."

"That's okay. I'll just wait on the porch."

Sharon and her husband let themselves in. A few seconds later I hear a scream. *What the hell?* I run inside after them.

"What is that?" Sharon shouts. "Is that blood?" She's pointing at the beige carpet, gripping her husband's arm. Spelled out in red letters is *I'm sorry*.

My stomach clenches, and my heart is pounding so hard I can feel it in my ears.

"Relax, Sharon," says Dave. "It's ketchup." He nods toward the kitchen, where a plain red ketchup bottle rests on the table. Then he bends down, sticks his finger in the bottom of the Y, and dabs his tongue with it. "Yep, definitely ketchup." He stands back up. "Owen!" he shouts, his voice booming.

Sharon runs up the stairs. "Owen? Olivia?" she says, moving room to room, her voice getting louder with each reiteration. "They're not here," she says shrilly, running back down the stairs.

"Probably at the store buying carpet cleaner. You want to give her a call?" Dave asks, looking at me.

"Sure." I fumble for my phone and tap Olivia's name. A ringtone I recognize chimes from the kitchen. I follow it to a phone with a zebra-striped case. "Um. This is Olivia's phone." I end the call. "And her Jeep is still here. So if they went anywhere, they must have walked."

"Right," he says. "Well, they'll probably be back any minute. Why don't you have a seat?"

"Thanks." I sit on the edge of an armchair, not wanting to get comfortable, trying to hide the deep breaths I'm taking.

"I'm sorry about the scream," Sharon says. "I kind of overreacted."

"Don't worry about it."

"Can I get you something to drink? A Coke, maybe?"

"Sure." I don't want anything, but it's obvious that Sharon wants something to do.

"Ice?"

"Please."

When Sharon brings me a glass, I take a nice long drink. "Hits the spot. Thanks."

"So how long have you and Olivia been dating?"

"Not long. I just moved here from Michigan."

"Oh. Did your dad get transferred?"

"No, he's a day trader. He's still back in Michigan. I'm living with my mom now."

"A day trader. Isn't that interesting! Does he do well?"

"Extremely." Enough so that he just took the new wife to Tahiti for two weeks, bought a house with a pool in Michigan and a condo in Colorado, and tried to bribe me with a new sports car.

"Ooh, sounds like we should be asking him for some stock tips, huh,

Dave?"

Dave doesn't answer. He's busy peering out the window.

I text Julia. **Have you seen Olivia?**

She texts back in less than a minute. **I think she's babysitting.**

She and Owen aren't here. Can you check with her other friends please?

Will do.

The more Sharon talks, the more nervous her voice sounds. Sharon keeps talking, asking me questions. Dave paces and peers. Fifteen minutes pass like this, then twenty. The whole time I'm fighting this about-to-puke feeling. *Come on, Olivia. Where are you?*

Finally Sharon says, "I'm going to call Olivia's mom. She probably knows where they are."

She disappears for a few minutes to the kitchen to make her call, leaving me and Dave alone, neither one of us wanting to talk.

Julia texts again. **No one has seen them. What's going on?**

Goose bumps break out on my arms.

Don't know. Will let you know when I find out.

"Olivia's mom hasn't heard anything. I'm calling the hospital," says Sharon, coming back into the living room with the phone in her hand.

Dave and I both stare at her as she makes the call.

When she shakes her head and says, "Not there," I'm both relieved and freaking out.

"So where do you think they are?" Dave looks at me uncertainly, as if he's hoping I'm going to give him the easy explanation he's been missing. But I have nothing. I shake my head. He pulls his keys out of his pocket. "I'll check the store and the park," he says decisively.

"I'm coming with you," says Sharon.

"No. Stay here in case they come back." Dave covers the distance from the dining room to the door in a couple of quick strides. "I'll take, what's your name, Jacob?"

"Yeah," I say, following behind him.

"Should I call the police?" Sharon asks.

"Call them," Dave says, flinging open the door. I have to sprint to keep up with him. He's backing out of the driveway before I can completely close the door. This guy doesn't mess around. He's going at least 40 in the neighborhood. I just hope he doesn't run over Olivia and Owen on their way home. Windows open, I study my side of the road while Dave scans his. "Is that them?" he asks, pointing to two figures on my side of the car.

I lean out the window, half my body sticking out. "Not them."

We continue to the grocery store. Dave pulls up right in front of the door. "Go," he says, shoving the car in Park and grabbing his keys out of the ignition.

I give the automatic door a push to help it open and jog from one side of the store to the other, examining each aisle as I blow past it. I cut some woman off. "Watch where you're going!" she says.

As I pass the next aisle, I catch a glimpse of Dave checking out the aisles from the back of the store. "Owen!" he belts out.

"Olivia!" I shout, surprised by the strength of my own voice.

As I work my way back to the exit, a store clerk blocks my way. "Is there something I can help you with?" he asks.

Dave comes up from behind and yanks me around the clerk. "They're not here," he says. "Let's go."

"No, thanks!" I shout over my shoulder at the clerk.

We jump back in the car and tear out of the parking lot. My head begins to pound. *Not now, not now.* I can't black out now. I press my hands against my temples and stick my head back out the window. *Focus!*

As Dave drives to the park, my mouth fills with saliva. *Damn it!* I'm going to throw up. Just hold it in. *Hold it in!*

I should have insisted she go to urgent care today, not waited for Monday.

What if she's passed out on a park bench? And there's no one to watch Owen. Shit.

We get out of the car at the park. There's the bridge where I held Olivia. Little kids are running across it now. Others are playing on the swings. "Owen! Olivia!" shouts Dave.

Spots form in front of my eyes. Every step seems like a mile. They're not here. *Why are they not here?*

I close my eyes. A memory rolls through me. My dad. Me. Where's Ben? We just closed our eyes for a few seconds. How could he be gone? "Ben!" I shout. "Ben!"

I feel a hand on my shoulder and open my eyes. It's Dave. "Owen," he says, his voice hoarse and shaky, his eyes watery. "My son's name is Owen."

"I know," I say softly. Then I run over to a bush and throw up.

Sixty

JACOB

When we get back to the house, a cop car and several others are parked in front.

Dave bursts through the front door and pans the room. "Are they back?" he asks hopefully.

There's a guy dusting for fingerprints in the living room and a woman taking pictures of the message on the carpet. A man in a suit sticks his hand out for Dave. "Mr. Webster? I'm Detective Montgomery. Your son and her babysitter haven't returned, but we're not ruling out the possibility that they simply went for a walk."

"The girl didn't take her cellphone with her. What teenager leaves that behind?"

Detective Montgomery breaks eye contact. "We are taking that into account."

My cellphone makes an annoying buzzing-beeping sound. And then all of the cellphones in the room erupt with the same tone.

"What is that?" Dave asks, his eyes darting about the room. "Is that an AMBER Alert?"

"It's just a precautionary measure," says Detective Montgomery.

Dave collapses into an armchair and mashes his hands through his hair. "Where's my wife?"

"She's upstairs with another detective in your son's room, checking to see if anything is missing. Perhaps a toy they might have taken outside to play with. When you're ready, Detective Morales can go with you out to the garage to see if there's anything missing there."

Dave jumps right up. "Of course. Sure. I can do that."

As Dave heads to the garage, Detective Montgomery turns to me. "And you are?"

"Jacob Brenner, Olivia's boyfriend. She's the babysitter."

"When did you first notice that Olivia was missing?"

"I was waiting for her at her mom's house. We had a date at four, and she wasn't back by four-thirty. I tried texting her, but she never answered. So I came over here. When she didn't answer the door, I looked around back. That was when the Websters got back. We went inside and saw the message on the carpet and Olivia's phone on the counter."

"That's when you went to look for them at the grocery store and the park? Do you remember which ones?"

"Yeah, it was the Savemart on Adams and…" I squeeze my eyes shut and try to think of the name of the park. "The park, it's the one a couple of blocks from here, over on Coral Street."

The detective writes the information in his notebook.

"Do you need the number for Olivia's mom?"

"Already got that from Mrs. Webster." He clicks his pen and stuffs it into his pocket. "What I'd like to do is have a patrol officer take you down to the station to get your fingerprints so we can isolate any prints here that don't belong."

This can't be happening. Where the fuck are they?

"Whatever you need. So you think they might have been kidnapped? Shouldn't you call the FBI? I can call my mom for you if you want. She works out of the Pittsburgh field office."

"You let me worry about the FBI. Now, if I could get you to go with Officer Stevens. He'll take down your contact information also. If I have any more questions, or an update, I'll give you a call. And here's my card in case you remember something."

"There is one thing. Olivia's been tired a lot lately. She falls asleep really easily. So it's possible they sat down somewhere and she fell asleep."

"Hmm, okay," he says noncommittally. I shake Detective Montgomery's hand, take his card, and follow Stevens, my thoughts in a fog and a million questions bouncing around inside my head. And as hard as I try, I can't push away that same helpless feeling that I had in my dream, when Olivia was plummeting from that cliff and I couldn't save her.

Screw Montgomery. As soon as I get into the squad car, I text my mom. **Olivia and Owen are missing. Please, you have to find them.** I add the Websters' address and hit Send.

My mom tries to call, but I reject the call and send her another text instead. **Can't talk now. Am fine. Just find them. Please.**

At the station Stevens leads me past a guy with wiry hair in handcuffs who's complaining loudly about his mother-in-law. A detective who looks like he's been up since yesterday is pouring coffee into a mug. We pass a few empty desks, another with a guy eating Cheetos, and one with a woman talking animatedly on the phone. *Get up, you people! Olivia and Owen are missing! Get up and look for them!* Finally, way in the bowels of the building, we arrive at the fingerprint machine, and the technician rolls my fingers. I turn to Stevens. "Just so you know, I was there once while my girlfriend was babysitting. So you might find my fingerprints a bit all over."

Officer Stevens nods. "I'll be sure to let the detective know."

When we're done at the station, Officer Stevens drives me back to the Websters' house. There are even more cars now than before. My mom's car is there too. And Aaron's. At least they're doing something. But it takes all of my concentration to stop from falling apart.

I consider going in and talking to my mom, but I'm afraid that I'll shake her and demand to know why they haven't found Olivia yet. *I'm not going inside. I'm going to go find them.*

Aaron probably thinks I had something to do with this.

Shit! Aaron said that Callaghan confessed to everything except Samantha's murder. *What if...God damn it! What if there really is a second killer out there?*

Please let it just be Olivia asleep on some park bench!

As I get in my truck and crank the engine, a javelin of pain spears my forehead.

No. Not again. I just need to keep going so I can find them!

I put the truck in gear and back up. Another javelin pierces my right temple. I accelerate, no destination in mind, following my gut. I go a few blocks, scanning for Olivia and Owen on the sidewalk. I turn left. Another two blocks and I turn right. On and on I go. The pain squeezes my head until my peripheral vision darkens to gray and to black. I miss a stop sign, and a car honks.

Must keep going.

Can't go any further. Must close eyes. Pull the knives out of my skull.

I stop the truck. I stumble out. Stagger in front of a car. Brakes squeal, and I stick my hand out. Slap my palm onto the black hood. Let the heat of the engine warm it. Feel the bumper as it presses against my leg.

"Watch out!" An angry old woman, with her white curls and round glasses, glares at me through the windshield. I push off from the hood and float the rest of the way across the street. I trip up gray stairs, open a door.

"Olivia! Owen!" I shout their names over and over, staggering from room to room. I knock over books, a plant, a glass of water. I keep going. *They must be here. They have to be.*

I reach the last room. Fling open the door. "Olivia? Owen?"

I think I must be whispering because no one answers.

I sink to my knees. Slide forward onto my stomach. Run my fingers along the wooden floor. My floor. My room. My house. My fault.

Sixty-One

JACOB

When I wake up, I'm still on the floor, but there's a pillow under my head and a blanket tucked carefully around my body. I look at the clock. Three a.m.

Shit! How did I lose so much time? I have to find them before it's too late.

I fumble for my phone and scroll through my texts and social media. Please let there be something from Olivia.

Nothing.

My headache is gone, but I'm still exhausted. From the glow of the phone, I notice a book under the bed. Probably that novel I'm supposed to read for English. Good thing I'm down here. I stretch my fingers and pull it out.

But it's not my English book. It's not a book at all. It's a journal. How did a journal get under my bed, and whose is it?

My skin prickles as I remember. After Olivia found my sketchbook, she was so upset that she picked up her backpack funny and everything spilled out. She must have missed this.

I turn on my bedside lamp, climb onto my bed, and open the cover. I don't intend to read it, at least I don't think I do. I trace my finger along the fancy swirls, then I close the book. I'm not going to read it. I feel the push and pull of two magnets. One makes me open the cover, the other makes me close it. Read. Don't read.

I read.

My dad used to tell me that there are people inside of marbles. They were always talking to him. Whenever I wanted to play a game, he would pick the one with marbles. Only, we wouldn't actually move the marbles. My dad would just stare at them.

I keep reading.

I read all of it.

My pulse throbs when she writes about our first kiss. Rage burns my face when she writes about the fire and her dad.

I don't believe her when she says she's just like him. She doesn't draw pictures of guns. She doesn't write *Kill Owen* or *Kill Jacob*. She's not like her dad.

She's not. All of this, what she heard or what she thought she heard. It has to mean something else.

I grab a piece of paper and a pen and make three lists.

Objects (things that Olivia heard voices coming from or that made her cold): Bird. Dolphin. Rock. Water fountain. Tunnel. Shaft. Medal. Bat. Stuffed animal. Rose. Bridge. River.

Words that Olivia heard (besides her name): Stop him. There's not much time. Counting. Ready or not.

Voices: Samantha's. A little boy's.

It has to mean something.

It has to.

I pace across my room, back and forth, back and forth. *Think!*

Four a.m. I'm not waiting any longer. I can't wait any longer. I flick on the hall light and march through the hall to my mom's room. I

213

knock on the door, but don't wait for her to answer before I go in. I turn the lamp on low and sit next to her as she wakes up. Aaron isn't here, which is good. Aaron doesn't believe in things he can't understand. "Mom? Mom, I need to show you something."

"Jacob? What is it? What's going on?" She scrambles to sit up. "What's the matter?"

"I need you to read this." I shove the journal into her hands. "It's Olivia's. I think it can tell us where they are if we can just figure it out." I read my list. "Bird. Dolphin. Rock. Water fountain. Tunnel. Shaft. Medal. Bat. Stuffed animal. Rose. Bridge. River. It's all in there."

"What is this? A journal?"

I nod, open to the first page, and wait for her to read.

First, she gets up and puts on her robe. "Make me some coffee, will you?" Then she goes to the living room, sits down on the couch, and reads. I sit next to her and try to figure out what she's thinking by what's written on her face, but she betrays nothing.

She looks up at me from time to time, but she reads the whole thing. Cover to cover. Then she closes the book.

"Well?" I ask. "Did you figure it out? Bird. Dolphin. Rock. Water fountain. Tunnel. Shaft. Medal. Bat. Stuffed animal. Rose. Bridge. River. They're clues. I know they're clues."

"I think you're right, Jacob. There are clues in this journal." She pulls me close to her. "But not the ones you think."

"What do you mean?"

"Jacob, we found their shoes. By the river." She kisses the top of my head. "We think they got swept up by the current and drowned. Olivia writes about hearing Samantha's voice calling her from the river, about getting in the river, about not wanting to get out. Honey, if I had to guess, I would say that Olivia heard Samantha's voice calling to her from the river, and this time she got in with Owen."

"No no no no no no no no!" I jump up and back away from the

couch. "You're wrong! Olivia did not drown herself! She did not! I don't believe it!"

"She probably tried to get out, but the current was just too strong. That necklace that she says she found in the river?"

"What about it?" I swallow hard. I remember that day, how out of it she was, how she was all wet, how she was wearing the necklace when she got back to her house. How I said it was pretty.

"Samantha's mother had told us that a butterfly necklace was missing, so when we found the necklace in Olivia's room we checked. It turns out that the necklace Olivia says she found actually belonged to Samantha."

"What are you saying?"

"I'm saying that maybe—just maybe—Olivia and Samantha had a fight. Maybe it got out of hand. Samantha ended up dead. Olivia made it look like it was the Sweet Dreams Strangler. But she couldn't deal with the guilt. She started hearing Samantha's voice."

"Damn it, Mom. That's not true. It can't be true."

I don't want it to be true.

But I'm afraid it might be.

There's a part of the journal that my mom didn't say out loud. Damning words that would have proven her point, words that now weigh on me as if someone had set an old car battery on my chest.

Before Olivia's dad set fire to the house where Olivia almost died, he left a suicide note in the car. While it rambled and raved and made little sense, one thing was clear. He was killing himself and his daughter to make the voices stop.

He also left a message on the car's windshield. It looked as if it had been written in blood, but it was actually written with ketchup.

It said, I'M SORRY.

Sixty-Two

JACOB

~⚬⚮⚬~

M y mom holds me, and I cry on her shoulder the same way I did the day my brother was gone. After all the tears have fallen and I'm left staring blankly at the wall in front of us, my mom gets up. "I'm going to take a quick shower, and then I need to take the journal with me. Show it to some people. You understand, right?"

"Yeah." I slump against the couch and wait for her to close the bathroom door. Then I pick up the journal, open to the most important pages, the pages with the real clues, not the fake ones that my mom thinks are important, but the real ones, the ones with the voices. I take pictures of the pages with my phone. I don't take a picture of the page with I'M SORRY because I know it's not a clue. But I do take a picture of the page with our first kiss. Just in case. So I can remember.

Sixty-Three

OLIVIA

wake up with a pounding headache. So cold. And damp. My eyes open, but the effect is the same as having them closed. I must still be sleeping. Wake up! As I shake my head, water drips on my face. I *am* awake. The air smells cold. Wet. My hands are numb—I must have fallen asleep on them. I sit up and reach for the light on my nightstand, but my hands won't move. It's almost as if they're tied together. I wiggle them back and forth. They *are* tied together. *Oh God, no.* The last memories I have aren't of going to bed. They're of following a bird with Owen, the river, someone's hand covering my mouth. My heart pounds. *Owen!* Where's Owen? I don't know whether or not to hope he's here.

Birds! Of course the last thing I remember would have something to do with birds! Did I just imagine that last bird, the one that drew us to the river? *No.* Owen saw it too, didn't he? He's the one who followed it. The birds, the voices, could they mean something else besides that I'm crazy?

Impossible. I shake my head and concentrate on the here and now. On what's real.

I try to shout, but only muffled grunts come out. A putrid tasting cloth is stuffed in my mouth. As my stomach heaves, I clamp my eyes shut and will the bile back down my throat. *If you vomit, you'll choke to death.*

I wiggle my toes. I can barely feel my feet, they're so cold. I vaguely remember someone taking off my shoes. No wonder my feet are cold. Struggling to stand, I teeter in a crouched position for a few seconds, then I slip and lose my balance, smacking my face against the floor, which is wet and hard and rocky. How could darkness be this dark? It's almost as if I'm in...

I'm in a cave! This is what it must be like to be buried underground. What if I never get out of here? A tickling feeling runs across my hand. A spider? *Oh God.* I scream involuntarily, but only a muted, smothered whine escapes.

Does cold have a smell? That's what I smell. Cold. Damp. Water. Wet. *I've got to get out of here.* I try to wriggle forward, but make almost no progress. The rope digs into my scar with an intensity that takes my breath away. I have to get it off. *Have to. Have to. Have to.*

Calm down, Olivia. Think. I slide around, feeling on the ground until I find a jagged piece of loose rock. *Yes!* I grasp it awkwardly and rub it against the ropes. I end up scraping my wrists more than the rope. *This is never going to work.* Even if it does, how will I find my way out of this cave? Without even a hint of light, how will I know which way is out and which way leads only deeper and deeper inside? And where is Owen? Why isn't he in here with me? Jacob said they found the Sweet Dreams Strangler. Did they arrest the wrong guy? If this is the Sweet Dreams Strangler, why would he take me when I was with Owen and not when I was alone? And if this isn't the Sweet Dreams Strangler, is Owen the one he wanted? Like the voice of the little boy that I kept hearing?

Please God, let Owen be okay!

My whole body hurts, as if I've been in a car accident. Or dragged through this cave against these rocks. My arms, my legs, even my jaw and nose throb. I keep working the rock against the ropes around my wrist, even though I'm cutting myself at the same time and blood is running down my arms.

The rock slips from my hands.

I'm never getting out of here.

I wallow for a few minutes, but then I picture the look of joy on Owen's face as he pumped his legs on the swing. *I have to get out of here! I have to find him!* I wrestle around on the ground until I find another rock, and I contine the scraping.

Damn it! I just sliced my wrist again. I grab it with my other hand to try to stop the bleeding and notice a slight give in the rope. *It's working!* I give up trying to stop the bleeding and instead keep up the scraping with the rock, back and forth, back and forth. My left arm, the one that I keep cutting, is feeling a little numb. I've got to stop. I need a break. I give it one last slice. It's still not enough.

Sixty-Four

JACOB

⁖⁖⁖

I study my three lists.

Objects: Bird. Dolphin. Rock. Water fountain. Tunnel. Shaft. Medal. Bat. Stuffed animal. Rose. Bridge. River.

Words: Stop him. There's not much time. Counting. Ready or not.

Voices: Samantha's. A little boy's.

I start with the dolphin. Olivia heard Samantha's voice after she saw me drawing dolphins all over my notes in class. The girl who was killed in Essex, she was wearing a dolphin shirt in the photo they showed on the news. Could the two be somehow related?

River. She found Samantha's necklace there, which could make it where Samantha was when she was taken. A river is also where the police found Olivia's and Owen's shoes. Is that the end of the story? Is that where the police will find their bodies?

No, damn it! Focus!

Rock. Could go with river. Rocks on the shore.

Tunnel. A river could seem like a tunnel. But what if was a real tunnel, like a tunnel through a mountain on the turnpike? Maybe whoever took them was heading that way in the car?

God, this is impossible!

Keep going, Jacob! You have to keep going! The answer is here somewhere. It has to be.

Bird. Obviously very important since she kept seeing them everywhere. But what could it mean. Flying?

Bat. What does baseball have to do with this? Maybe training camps? Florida? Were they taken on a plane to Florida?

Bird, bat. What if *bat* wasn't baseball bat? What if it was bat, as in the flying animal? I flip through the journal pages in my phone to the entry about laser tag. Olivia heard a voice coming from a rock wall. Which was made to look like a cave. What if this isn't about baseballs and rocks? What if it's about a cave?

Olivia was freaking out when we went to the cave. Especially at the end, when that guy was helping her into the climbing gear. What was that guy's name? Could this have something to do with him?

Think! There was a flyer! When we signed up for the trip, there was a flyer! But where is it now? I grab my backpack and dump the contents onto the bed. I pick up the folders and shake the papers out, then I leaf through them, discarding the useless ones on the floor. Not there. I take all of the textbooks and shake them upside down, grabbing the papers that fall out.

What if I folded it up and put it in my pocket? If it went through the wash, I'm screwed. But if I took it out and put it on my dresser...

There is one square of paper on my dresser. My hands shake as I unfold it.

This is it.

The guy in charge, he was Jeff Wilson. But the other guy, the one who helped Olivia with her gear, was Kevin Shipman. And I'm one Google search away from finding out where he lives.

Sixty-Five

JACOB

$\sim\!\!\infty\!\!\sim$

My phone tells me that I'm at Shipman's house, though all I can see is a pebbled driveway leading into the woods. I consider the direct approach but quickly realize it for what it is—just plain stupid. If this guy isn't a kidnapper, he'll think I'm crazy, and if he is, the moment he realizes I'm a threat to his plan, I'll be dead. So I continue past the house and turn down the next road I find. After parking my truck on the side of the road, I walk back to Shipman's property, careful to avoid the driveway. It isn't difficult to do, and I feel pretty confident that I'm invisible to the house, which is surrounded by acres of trees and isolated from any neighbors. I'm circling the house, planning an approach from the back, when I hear the faint babble of a stream.

Although I feel pulled in two directions, both toward the house and the sound of the water, I feel the pull of the water stronger. I follow the slope of the land down, farther and farther until I reach the water's edge where the sound of the water fills my ears so completely that if Shipman were to sneak up behind me, I would never hear him. I wonder for a moment if my mom was right—if Olivia and Owen did disappear into the water. Only, what if they didn't disappear into it, but only with it? I continue my perusal of the shore, searching for some type of boat, though I know that would be too easy. If someone had taken them with a boat, it was most certainly now in some sort of garage or outbuilding. As I clamber about the rocky terrain, a break in the rock, a darkness, captures my attention. I have to duck to see it properly and crawl to gain entry, but what I see in front of me is none other than the entrance to a cave.

Sixty-Six

OLIVIA

I think I must have drifted off. It's still so dark. Panic bubbles up from my toes to my legs to the tips of my fingers to the back of my neck. *I have to get out of here!* With no idea how much time has passed, I'm now completely starving, and the gag in my mouth seems almost dry. Is this guy even coming for me, or is he just going to leave me in this cave to starve to death? And what about Owen?

When he was chasing the bird, Owen said, "There it is again." Has this person tried to get him to follow the bird before? Did Samantha see the guy who was flying it? Is that why she was killed?

I feel around on the ground for the rock, knowing that the longer I wait, the less strength I'll have for getting myself out of here. I move the rock back and forth against the ropes with considerably less energy than before. *What did Jacob think when I didn't show up for our date? And my mom, she must be completely freaking out.* I slam the rock down again, twisting and pressing as though squashing a hideous, furry-footed tarantula.

And finally it works! I'm free!

I rub my wrists, wiping the fresh blood on my jeans and wincing as the material brushes against other cuts and my scar, sending a rippling, tugging sensation up my arm. Although I know I should free my feet first so I can get the hell out of here, I can't bear to leave the gag in one minute longer. It's so tight that there's no way I can get it out without first loosening it. All I want to do is pull and yank and be free of this horrid, disgusting thing, but I know that will just make it tighter. I dig desperately under the knots until my arms feel so heavy that they drop and a silent scream pulses inside of me. Again. Over and over again I tease the knots.

Yes! The ends are free. As I pull the gag out, the dryness of my mouth acts like glue, and I'm afraid for a minute that it won't come out. But it does. I try to scream, to yell, but only a small whimper comes out. I swallow repeatedly. Now for my feet. I pick at the knots, but instead of the instant freedom I had hoped for, I find it to be a dizzying, difficult process without the use of my eyes. I feel for the rock, now almost a friend, and I start to saw.

And then I hear a voice. "Olivia?"

No! That's Jacob's voice! It can't be real. There's no way Jacob could have found me. Just further proof that I'm crazy.

Or that Jacob is…dead.

Please let me be crazy.

Sixty-Seven

JACOB

⚬⚭⚬

"Olivia!" I shout. I give up trying to be quiet. If Shipman is in here, so be it.

Drip. Drip. All I hear is the trickle of water. No way she's here. No way she's even on the property. What was I thinking? I switch on the flashlight app on my phone and keep moving anyway. The farther I go, the narrower the walls and the lower the roof of the cave. The air feels heavy and wet. I shiver. Should have brought a jacket. *This is stupid, Jacob. Olivia is dead. She drowned herself. Owen too.*

But if she didn't and her voices were real, then there was one that was undeniable.

The counting. *Ready or not.*

Both part of hide-and-seek.

Both spoken in a little boy's voice.

My brother's voice. Ben's.

Bent over and making slow progress, I come to a fork in the path.

My instinct is to go right, but probably only because I'm right-handed. I hesitate. *Make a decision, Jacob!* I go right. I hunch over more and more until I'm crawling. This is crazy. I should just turn around. Get out of the cave completely. I'm crawling, the rock rough on my hands. Although I know this is pointless, I keep chugging along, keep wanting to believe that my mom, the police, the whole damned FBI, that they're all wrong. The pain from my hands scraping against the rocks feels almost good. It takes away some of the pain I'm feeling on the inside.

I push my way through the pain, faster and faster until I'm not cold anymore but actually sweating, and then I lift my right hand and set it down again—only it doesn't smack down into the rock. It falls down into nothing, into a big hole of nothingness, and I fall flat on my chest. My palm opens and the phone that I had been gripping tumbles from my hand. I lunge forward, snatching the air, trying desperately to grab it, but all I get for my trouble is a nasty scrape on my stomach that burns as my skin is scraped away. After a bit there's a plop as my phone hits the water, way too far down to reach without falling in. As the phone sinks, the flashlight app continues to shine, revealing nothing but a sheer drop and water in front of me.

I have to go back, but there isn't enough space to turn around. The only way is to back out. Already the light is fading; whether because of how deep the phone is submerged or because the water has sucked the life out of it, I don't know, and it doesn't matter. I begin the arduous task of crawling backward.

"Jacob?"

The dark must be playing tricks on my mind because I thought I heard...

"Jacob?"

The voice is a little louder this time, but still far away, and I can't tell where it's coming from. The voice is raspy. It doesn't sound like her, but who else could it be?

"Olivia?"

"Yes! It's me!"

Oh God. It sounds like she's on the other side of the water. Or is that the echo? I can't tell.

"Where are you?" I shout.

"Some sort of room. It feels big."

"Are you near the water?"

"I don't know. I don't think so."

I let out my breath. Behind. She's definitely behind me. *Thank God.* I power backward as fast as I can with renewed energy. I can't believe she's here. I can't believe she's alive! I can't...my stomach plunges. "Is Owen with you?" I try not to let the panic show in my voice.

"I'm not sure." Her voice wavers. "But I don't think so."

"It's okay. We'll find him," I say, determined. By now my knuckles and palms must be bloody, my jeans and shirt are ripped, but I don't feel anything, just a hopeful numbness. Finally I reach the fork, this time choosing the other path.

"Jacob?"

"Yeah?" *Good.* Her voice is clearer now. This must be the right way.

"Are you really here? You're not dead, are you? Because lately I've been hearing voices. From dead people. So I'm really hoping you're not dead."

"I know about your voices. I read everything. But I'm one hundred percent alive, and we're going to be together any minute."

"Thank you, Jacob. I don't know how you did it, how you knew how to find me, but thank you."

"It was all you. Your journal. The voices you heard. They were all clues. Almost everything makes sense. Except for the birds. I haven't figured that part out yet."

"It's how he got Owen to follow him. A toy. Some kind of remote control bird. Jacob, I'm so scared. Where is Owen? What has he done with Owen?"

"Don't worry. We're going to find him."

"Where is everyone? Why don't I hear anyone else? Are they looking for Owen?"

They're looking for him. Just not here. They're dragging the bottom of the river. But I can't tell her that. "They will be. As soon as I can call them. But first let's get you out of here."

This time I feel the edge of nothingness before I do another chest plant. "Olivia?"

"Yes? I'm over here. I think you're in the same room now."

I can't see a thing. I lean over the edge as far as I can, but I can't feel the ground.

I've found her prison. But how far down is she? And if I jump, will we ever make it out?

Sixty-Eight

OLIVIA

Jacob is near. Very near. I can feel it. "Where are you?" I ask.

"Right here. I'm up on some kind of ledge. You're lower than I am. Try to follow my voice."

Follow his voice. I've had a lot of practice with following voices. Too much. "I haven't been able to get my legs free, but I think I can do it by hopping." I push off against the floor and bring myself into a standing position. I hop across what seems like a room while Jacob keeps calling out "This way…over here." After several hops, I lose my balance and fall, landing on my right arm. "Damn it."

"You okay?"

"I'll be fine." I push myself back up and continue, getting closer and closer until finally I reach a wall. "This must be it. This must be your ledge," I say. "I can feel the wall, but not the ledge. It's gotta be above my head."

"Here. I'm going to drop my Swiss army knife down for you to cut the rope around your legs. That way you'll also know exactly where I am. But back up a bit first so it doesn't hit you."

"Just give me a second." I pivot and take several hops back. "Okay. Go ahead."

Even though it doesn't make a difference whether my eyes are open or closed since I can't see anything either way, I close my eyes and wait for the sound of the knife falling.

Thunk.

"Okay. I've got to go a little to the left." I take one hop left and drop to the ground, feeling all around. Nothing. I drag my knees more left, then more forward, until I hit the wall again. I pull at my hair in frustration. *We have to get out of here!* Every second that I waste looking for this knife is a second that sicko has with Owen.

"Keep trying," Jacob encourages.

I keep moving, keep feeling, keep… "There it is!" I shout, relieved.

Although I've used a Swiss army knife before, I've never tried using one without being able to see. I run my fingers over a smooth surface, then try to guess which of the ridged tools is the knife. The first thing I manage to pull out is a scissors, but I know I'm going to need something much sharper to break through the rope. Next I find the little magnifying glass, then a flathead screwdriver and then, just as I'm ready to give up and use the scissors, a knife. I place the blade on the rope between my two feet and begin to saw. Back and forth, back and forth. Will we ever get out of here? Tears spring to my eyes. Finally the cord snaps free. "Got it!" I close the knife and put it in my pocket, then rub my ankles and stand up. "Now what?"

"I'm going to reach down as far as I can. You reach up and try to grab my hand."

I flatten myself against the wall and stretch as tall as I can, balancing on my tiptoes.

"Where are you?"

"Here."

I sweep my hand all along the wall. Nothing. My heart plummets. "It's no use. You must be too high up. You should go get help. I'll be fine. You've got to get the police here to look for Owen anyway."

"Let's try one more thing. Try jumping to see if you can reach my hand that way."

"Okay. Here I go." I jump, my hands above my head, straining as far as they will reach. All I find is air. My bare feet sting from smacking against the ground.

"Again," says Jacob.

On my fourth jump my fingers graze Jacob's hand. "That was it!" I say.

"Can you check and see if there are any foot holes you can use on the wall, any places where the wall juts out a bit?"

"Just a minute." I feel along the bottom edge of the wall. "Here. I think there's something I can work with here."

"Great! As you jump, try to push off against that rock. I'll grab your hands, and you see if you can walk your way up the wall until I can pull you up."

"Here goes nothing," I say. I step back a few paces so I can get a running start and then go for it. I'm able to use the rock for leverage, but then tumble down before reaching Jacob's hand. "Let me try again."

"You can do it," Jacob says. I step back even farther this time, run, leap. Strong hands grip mine, pulling me upward. I use the momentum from my running start and some outcropping of rock to propel myself steadily up the wall until I'm far enough up to fling my arms onto the ledge. Jacob grabs my belt loops and drags me the rest of the way up. I'm so elated to be out of my cave room that I'm able to block out most of the pain from the friction burns and scrapes.

Jacob collapses on the rock floor, pulling me on top of him. I rest my head on his chest, listening to the wild beating of his heart. After a bit I search with my hands for Jacob's face, and he does the same to mine. I go for a kiss and end up planting one on his eyelid. It's nice, but I manage to land the next one on his lips, and it's better.

"I can't believe you found me," I say. "How did you…?"

"Your journal. It was all in your journal."

"The only thing in my journal is evidence that I'm crazy."

"The water, the bat…The bat, that was my brother trying to tell you about the cave." Jacob plays with a strand of my hair.

My breath catches. "Your brother?"

Jacob reaches for my right hand, then puts both of his hands around mine and squeezes gently. "He…my brother…" Jacob's voice cracks. "He disappeared when he was about the same age as Owen."

"What?" I place my cheek against Jacob's.

"Hide-and-seek? You know, all of the things you heard—the counting, the 'ready or not'—they're both from a game of hide-and-seek."

With my free hand, I stroke Jacob's face.

"We were playing hide-and-seek when he was taken." His voice catches on the last few words.

"But that would mean…"

"That my brother's dead? Yeah." Jacob squeezes my hand again and rubs my palm. "In my heart I think I knew it all along, but when I found out that you heard that voice…and it started while I was holding you, well, I knew it just had to be him."

"I'm so sorry. I didn't know…"

"Of course you didn't."

As Jacob and I kiss one more time, I can taste his sorrow. We get up slowly, holding hands, and my fear drifts away.

"Who was it, Jacob? Who took us?"

"Kevin Shipman. He was in that cave when we went on the field trip. The guy who helped you put on your gear. He has a house in the middle of the woods, complete with his own cave."

"My God. I can't believe I didn't know, that I didn't figure this out." I stumble backward. Jacob's grip tightens, preventing me from falling. "So you think, because of your brother, you think that this guy was after Owen, not me?"

"It looks that way."

"Well then, we've got to find him, we've got to get to Owen as soon as we can!"

"I agree. Are you okay to walk?"

"I'm fine."

"This way then," he says, tugging my hand and maneuvering us through the seemingly impossible maze. How does he remember which way to turn? What if he gets it wrong? We might be trapped in here forever.

The minutes flow by, and we seem no closer to getting out than when we started. I swallow hard and try to stay calm. Just one badly bruised foot in front of the other, one foot in front of the other.

"Do you need to take a break?" Jacob asks.

"No. Let's keep going. Are you sure we're going the right way?"

He doesn't answer immediately. "Pretty sure." He squeezes my hand. "Come on, we'll be out of here before you know it!"

On and on we trudge, and with each step my stomach sinks lower and lower until I want to fall down on my knees and give up. Each time I'm tempted, I think about how Jacob risked everything to come find me and how we have to keep going for Owen.

"Light! Do you see that light up ahead?" I ask, amazed.

"I see it, Olivia. We're almost out of here!"

As we get closer to the light, our steps quicken. "Oh my God, we're out! We're finally out!" The sun is so bright and my eyes so unaccustomed to it that I'm almost as blind in the daylight as I was in the darkness, but relief and gratitude fill me up inside.

As we take our first steps outside, Jacob pauses, squinting and shading his eyes with one hand. "My truck is down the street a ways. We should probably take it and go get help. Oh God, your feet. Here, let me carry you."

"I'm okay to walk. And we've got to find Owen first. If that maniac, that Kevin Shipman realizes that I'm missing, who knows what he'll do with Owen. But where are they? Besides the house, there are all these outbuildings. Where do we even start?"

"Wait a minute." Jacob is staring intently at the house.

"What is it?"

"What kind of plants are those around the house?"

"You mean the rose bushes?"

"When I gave you the rose, before the dance, you were cold."

I shudder as I realize that Jacob is right. "That's where he is, isn't it?"

"I think it's our best shot, but we need to find a way into the house that doesn't involve ringing the doorbell. I say we go around back and try to get in through one of the windows. Unless you have a better idea?"

I shake my head. "No. Let's go."

Jacob grabs my hand once again and sets off toward the house, moving us quickly from behind one tree to the next until we're right behind the house. All of the curtains are drawn, and it's not dark enough to need lights on indoors, so it's impossible to see what's inside. Jacob draws near a window on one of the corners. If we're lucky, this is the room that Owen's being held in and we could be in and out without his captor even noticing. Just as likely, I figure, is the possibility that we'll walk right into a trap.

Jacob reaches for the window.

I breathe in the stench of stale cigarettes. "What's that—" An arm slams into my neck and grips tightly, making it nearly impossible to breathe. A cold, round metal object digs into my temple.

No! Panic shoots up my legs and arms. *No, this can't be happening.*

Jacob got me out of the cave. All we need to do now is to get Owen.

As Jacob whips around, Kevin says, "Don't do anything stupid. Move it! Into the house, both of you!"

Jacob balls his fists, and for a moment I think he's going to try to jump Kevin, but instead he unfurls his palm. "Calm down, man."

Kevin's grip on my neck tugs me backward, so moving forward feels like I'm walking uphill.

Kevin nudges me with the gun into the house. I stumble over the threshold and crash into an end table, knocking off a pack of cigarettes. A lighter teeters on the edge. I grab hold of the table to catch my balance.

Samantha's voice is coming from the lighter. *Fire.*

"Well, isn't this cozy?" says Kevin.

I'm hungry! Another voice is coming from a bookshelf across the room. Damn it! I cover my ears, as if it will do any good. I have to think.

"Owen!" Jacob shouts, picking up a video baby monitor from the bookshelf. That voice was real. That voice was…

"That stuffed animal…that's my brother's!" Jacob says incredulously.

Kevin shrugs. "It's been quite popular with the boys."

Fire. Start a fire.

"You were…you must have been the…I remember you! You were the guy who used to mow the park. Where is he? Where's my brother? Is he here?"

Fire.

Jacob's cheeks redden, his eyes blaze, and he looks as if he's about to whip the monitor at Kevin. The only thing stopping him is the gun pointed at his chest.

"Oh, you didn't think I kept them for myself, did you?" Kevin gives a self- satisfied grin, staring right at Jacob. "You know, you really shouldn't close your eyes when you're playing hide-and-seek with a little kid. But thanks for that. Polite kid, your brother. Tell your mom she did a real good job with that please and thank you thing. Oh, that's right," he says, rubbing his chin with his free hand, "you're never going to see her again." He shrugs. "Your parents really should have kept a better eye on their kids. That's two for two now. Actually, Ben I did keep for myself. Not on purpose. He was a wily little fellow. Got himself free. Ran into the cave. Had an unfortunate accident. Well, enough chitter chatter. Owen and I have places to go, people to see. And you two are in the way." Kevin glances at me. "Pity your boyfriend had to show up. The papers would have had such a compelling story: teen follows in her father's footsteps, drowning child, self in murder-suicide—bodies never found. Now we'll have to revise the narrative to include one more."

Fire. Fire. Fire. Fire. Fire.

Kevin pulls back the safety on the gun and moves toward Jacob. He's not going to wait. He's going to kill Jacob right now!

Fire fire fire fire fire fire fire.

I can't think. I can't do anything. Samantha's voice has to stop.

I grab the lighter, knocking over the end table.

Kevin's eyes shift from Jacob to me. But he doesn't see the lighter behind my back.

My palms are so sweaty the lighter nearly slips out of my fingers.

I will not start a fire. That would be crazy. Stupid. I won't do it. I can't do it. There is nothing that I hate more, nothing that frightens me more than...

Fire fire fire fire fire fire fire fire fire fire.

I can't do it. I won't.

Kevin is staring at me. He hasn't yet figured it out. How could he? The lighter is behind my back. Besides, I'm not doing it. I can't. I won't. Never. No one can make me.

Fire.

Never.

Fire fire fire.

I pull my hand from behind my back.

I flick the lighter.

The flame jumps and dies out.

I take a few paces. Kevin starts toward me. He's almost here.

Last chance.

It's not me. I'm not doing this. It's not my fault. It's Samantha's. Why won't she leave me alone?

I plant my hand right under the curtain.

I flick the lighter again. The flame jumps to life, biting, attacking, devouring the bottom edge of the curtain.

What have I done?

"Fire." It's my voice, not Samantha's. It's quiet, not loud. Just a whisper, really.

I can't have done it. I would never do it. I don't believe in fire. Fire frightens me, it terrifies me, the fear of it consumes me.

I drop the lighter.

For a moment nobody moves. Then the gun goes slack in Kevin's hand as he springs into action. He grabs a book from a shelf and starts beating the curtains, trying to stop the flames from spreading.

Yes! Stop them! Fire is bad. Fire is evil. I didn't want the fire. Not then. Not now. No. Never. *Daddy, no!*

For a moment it works, and the flames get smaller, and there's just smoke, but then they spring to life with renewed vigor, and they slither their way up the curtain, dancing, taunting, playing, burning, and pages of the book catch fire, and the book must be hot because Kevin drops it and, along with it, drops the gun.

Sixty-Nine

JACOB

He's waving that book around like crazy when he drops the gun. I try to grab it, but Shipman lands a kick to my shin and then a right hook to my face. Olivia tries to snatch up the gun, but Shipman kicks her and then seizes her hair. I snatch one of his legs and yank. He kicks at my face, but I hang on with everything I have left. Finally he loses his balance and releases Olivia's hair.

"Go! Get Owen!" I shout. "I got this!" I tug his leg again, and down he goes.

Right on top of me.

Seventy

OLIVIA

⁓❦⁓

I run down the hallway, flinging open all the doors. "Owen! Where are you? Owen?"

Why is he not answering me? How can he not hear me? A fire? What was I thinking? Why would I ever listen to a voice in my head? Oh my God, I had a knife in my pocket, Jacob's Swiss army knife. I could have used the knife! There was no need to start the fire. Would the knife have been enough? If I had charged Kevin with the knife, would it all be over now? Or would he have shot one of us as I charged?

"Owen!"

I'm not going to think about the fire. I can't think of the fire. If I think about it, I won't move. I'll be stuck in this place forever. Owen will die. Jacob will die. We will all die.

It will be my fault.

The air is hazy and smoky. I cough. Heat rises. I should be crawling, but I'm not. It would take too long. I have to run.

"Owen!" He's not here. Not on this floor. Wait! One more door. The basement.

I flick the light on and rush the stairs.

Time. No time. Out of time.

I gallop down the stairs. The air here is still cool, still unblemished by the fire. My fire.

"Owen!"

Still nothing. How is that possible? He has to be here. There is no other place, is there?

I pull on a string hanging from the ceiling. A single bulb illuminates rows of shelves, neatly arranged. Glass jars of peaches, pineapple in cans, laundry detergent, napkins. But no Owen.

Damn it. Tears spring to my eyes. What have I done? I speed past all of the jars and slap my hand against the wall. It's hard, cold, concrete. I run my hands up and down and along the wall until I reach the corner. "Owen!" The farther I go, the darker it gets, and the harder it is to breathe. Not because of the smoke—it hasn't reached here yet—but from the futility of what I'm doing. And then...is it? Could it be? The wall feels different. Not as cold. It feels like a wall that could be in a living room...or a bedroom. It's too dark to see any sort of door, but my hands find a hole, dime-sized, and then a button, like a doorbell. I push it and hear a click.

A door without a handle swings open. It's the room from the monitor. "Owen! Thank God!" Owen looks up, startled. The walls have a puffy look to them, as does the inside of the door, no doubt some sort of soundproofing.

"Where did you go?" Owen asks. "Why did you leave me with the mean guy?" he accuses, running into my arms. I hug him, whisking him into the air at the same time. I have to get him out of this room, out of this house. Out of this nightmare.

Seventy-One

JACOB

The fall with Kevin takes my breath away. The weight on my chest is crushing, and the sharp pain tells me I have at least one broken rib. Face up, I watch the flames jump from the curtains to a nearby lampshade. Smoke is gathering in thick, puffy clouds near the ceiling. My throat stings, and I cough. Kevin landed on my left side, so I roll quickly and wrestle my way out from underneath him. As I stand, I see a phone on the kitchen wall and dive for it. I grab it and dial 911. Kevin charges. As I push the button to connect, Kevin plows into me, knocking the phone to the ground. He slams me into the counter, where a stack of plates slides to the floor, shattering.

"911. What is your emergency?"

I'm coughing pretty steadily now, but I shout "Fire!" as loud as I possibly can. "This is Jacob Brenner. My mom works for the FBI. There's a kid and a guy with a..."

My coughing prevents me from finishing my sentence, but it doesn't matter since Kevin retrieves the phone, hangs up, and tosses it. I search desperately for a weapon. *Knives, where are the knives?* There's no wooden block on the counter. I open drawers at random, then cabinets. Finally I see something I can use—what looks like a cast iron skillet. I reach for it, and my fingers touch the rough handle long enough to confirm what it is, but I'm yanked backward before my hand can close around it.

Kevin shoves me to the floor again, this time in complete control, with one hand clutching my neck. My head throbs from the smack against the floor, and as I look above me, I see little spots mixed in with the clouds of smoke. I'm already dizzy from the smoke and the blows to the head, but when his hands squeeze my throat and my own hands are firmly pinned by his knees, I realize that my only hope is to play dead and hope that he stops squeezing before I really am dead.

I close my eyes and try to lose myself in the spinning motion of the merry-go-round in my head, but this is a thousand times worse than I thought it would be. It takes everything I have to not squirm, to not try to fight back. I'm drowning and holding my breath and choking all at the same time, and I'm thinking that maybe this wasn't the best idea because I think I'm dying now. I try to fight back, only the messages my brain is sending my hands aren't getting there and I feel myself drifting away and I think I see my brother's face in one of the clouds and the next thing I know I'm running, only not on the ground, but in the air.

Seventy-Two

OLIVIA

I run up the stairs with Owen in my arms. As we reach the top, the oppressive smoke makes us both cough.

"What's going on?" Owen asks as I put him down. "Why is it hard to see?"

"There's a fire, but we're going to be just fine. We're going to crawl to the bedroom back here. Follow me." I keep one shoulder to the wall and follow it to the first doorway on the right, a bedroom I saw when I was looking for Owen. "This way, Owen, to the right." Once we're in the room, I move as quickly as I can to the window and fling it open. Then I fumble with the latches to the screen and raise it. "Okay, Owen, I need you to climb out the window and go stand by that tree over there. I have to go help my friend Jacob find his way out. I need you to promise me that you won't come back in the house. No matter what. Do you understand me? Sit by the tree and wait for the firemen. Can you do that, buddy?"

Owen nods, coughing too hard to talk. I lift him over the sill. "Now

244

jump down and run!"

Please make him stay outside.

I leave the bedroom, terrified about what I'll find in the living room. Is Jacob okay? Suddenly I realize that Kevin could already be outside. What if he sees Owen? Maybe I should stay with him. I hesitate. No. I have to try to find Jacob. I stand but hunch over, trying to stay out of the smoke. I feel my way toward the living room. "Jacob? Jacob? Are you still inside? Are you okay? Jacob?"

Oh God, why isn't he answering?

As I reach the living room, a figure faces me. "Jacob?" I whisper hopefully, knowing in my heart it's not him.

Bang!

Seventy-Three

JACOB

Bang!

I open my eyes, expecting to see a gun pointed at me. The room is hazy, but I don't see a gun. My throat hurts like hell. I need to cough, but I'm afraid to. Afraid of the pain, afraid of...what am I afraid of exactly? I know it's important. If I could just remember.

Shit! You can't cough because you're supposed to be dead. I pretended to be dead so that guy would stop squeezing my throat. I must have passed out. If the gun didn't hit me, it must have hit someone, it must have hit...

Olivia! That bastard must have shot Olivia! Or Owen. Or both.

I look down at my hand. I was reaching for something right before... What was I reaching for? A series of images parades through my head. A lighter. Curtains. The kitchen. Being shoved into a counter. Knives. Looking for knives. No knives.

A skillet! A cast iron skillet! That's what I was trying to grab when Kevin tackled me. Where is it? Is it still in the cabinet where I saw it?

I roll to my stomach and crawl across the tile floor. Yes! The skillet is still there. I grip it and rise unsteadily to my feet. I turn and stumble to the living room. By the time I get there, Shipman is already out the front door. Olivia is dragging herself across the room.

"Olivia! Are you okay? Are you shot?"

"Yeah, but I'll be okay. I can get myself out. You have to stop him! I sent Owen out there. You can't let him take Owen! I'm fine. I'll be right behind you. And if not, you'll come back for me. You have to get Owen first! Go!"

I rush the door and run down the porch steps. Where is he? I circle around to the back. That's when I see Owen, eyes covered, hiding behind a tree, believing as only a child can that if he can't see anyone, no one can see him. Shipman is headed toward Owen, is almost there. I charge him, nearly reaching him as he touches Owen's shoulder. Shipman whips around, gun pointed at me. It's hard to tell which one of us reacts first. He fires and I swing the skillet, letting the momentum of my swing carry me to the side as the bullet continues forward, hitting no one. Kevin falls, out cold, at least for the moment. I grab his gun, engage the safety, and force it into my front pocket.

"Olivia?" *Damn it, I thought she was right behind me.* I point at Shipman's pickup in the driveway. "Owen, I need you to get in that truck and lock the door. Can you do that?"

Owen nods.

"That's my buddy." As Owen runs toward the truck, I run for the front porch. Smoke is billowing through the screen door. I use the bottom of my shirt to turn the metal doorknob, but as I step through the doorway, huge flames block my path. I try stepping one way and then the other, but nothing works. There's no way I can get in this way. I swallow hard as bile rises to my throat. Is Olivia in those flames? Is it already too late? "Olivia! Olivia! Can you hear me?"

Nothing. Damn it.

I rush back to the truck. "Owen!" I shout at the window. "How did you get out of the house? Did you go through the front door?"

Owen shakes his head. "The back window," he shouts, pointing.

I follow his finger and run to the window. Smoke is coming out of this window, but it's not as intense as the front door, and I'm able to climb in.

Seventy-Four

OLIVIA

~~~

I'm standing at the edge of a cliff. It looks like the Grand Canyon. I'm not sure why I'm here or where I've been. All I know is that I'm here now. A bunch of people are lined up next to me. Our toes all graze the edge. I have this great urge to jump, and no matter how much I try to talk myself out of it, it does no good.

I jump.

"No! Olivia, no!" All of a sudden Jacob is in the air next to me. His arms are up, as if he's trying to fly.

"Jacob!" Even though I'm falling, I'm grinning like crazy.

"Like this, Olivia! Put your arms like this!"

I copy him, but it doesn't do any good. I'm still falling. He reaches out and grabs both of my hands. He hangs on tight, too tight even. But somehow my hands slip out anyhow. He flies upward.

And I slam into the ground.

Someone is shaking my arm. "Olivia, it's me. Wake up, it's me."

I open my eyes.

It's Samantha. "Hey girl," she says. She puts her hand on my forehead. She smiles wistfully. "I guess I should say, 'Welcome.'"

I try to sit up. "Not too fast. Just rest a bit," she says.

My eyes feel heavy. I lie back down. The sun is shining brightly. Birds are singing, but sweetly, softly. Somehow I don't mind them. "But this means…I must be…"

"Yeah," she says simply. "You are."

"Thanks for trying," I say. I can barely keep my eyes open. Samantha's face shimmers in front of me.

"My pleasure. It wasn't easy, you know."

"Is that why you were always shouting?" I murmur.

She laughs and clasps both my hands. A warm, soothing, pulsing feeling overtakes me. "Is that the way it sounded? I guess I was just worried you couldn't hear me."

"That was just me trying to ignore you. Sorry about that."

"You mean the way I ignored you when I was still alive?"

"I guess we're even then. Friends?" I say.

She squeezes my hand. "Friends," she answers.

"You know, I'm pretty tired. I think I need to close my eyes for just a minute."

"Take all the time you need," she says.

I let my eyes drift shut.

Seventy-Five

JACOB

As soon as I'm through the window, I drop to my knees, trying to draw on my practically nonexistent fire safety skills. I remember something about trying to cover your mouth and nose with a cloth. I think it's supposed to be wet. With no towels in sight, I whip off my shirt. It's wet enough from sweat. I slap it against my mouth and try to breathe through my nose. It's hard to do because I'm pretty much coughing constantly. When I do manage to, I inhale the pungent stench of sweat, or perhaps I only imagine it in my desperate struggle to distract myself from the fire that is quickly overtaking this house. I cross the room on my knees in what I think is a straight line, but when I reach the other side, I hit a wall instead of a doorway. Smoke is hanging so heavy in the room that my eyes, in the moments I'm able to open them, are useless.

I slide my hands along the wall, frantically searching for the doorway. When I finally find it, I nearly tumble out into the hallway. Once I'm clear, I pull the door closed behind me. That will help keep the fire out of that room, won't it?

Right. I need to go right. I move into the hall, my right arm pressed against the wall so I don't get disoriented and start wandering the wrong way. "Olivia!" I try to shout, but I can barely hear my own voice. "Olivia!"

I pass a gap in the wall. Must be another bedroom. I keep going. Another gap. How long is this hallway? Finally there is a gap that doesn't end. I feel the change in the floor too, from the hardwood of the hallway to the softness of carpet. This has to be the living room. The room where the fire started, where the flames must be the most intense. Where I left Olivia. My head fills with a crackling sound. It sounds almost like running water, or maybe I just hear it that way because I'm so desperate for cool water running over my arms, cool water pouring down my throat.

Wait. Where am I? Am I asleep? This dream sucks. I just need to get back to sleep, back to a better dream. My head feels all swirly and sleepy. I think I'll just…

Bam! What was that? Shit, this is no dream. This is a fire. This is real. I have to find Olivia. I have to get her out of here. I move across the floor, my arms sweeping the floor, searching for her, not finding her. Where is she?

Crack! Something drops to the floor. Orange, glowing. It lights up the room long enough for me to see her. "Olivia!" I stand, and with an energy I didn't know I had, I rush over to her and scoop her into my arms. But it's hard and at first I lose my grip. Her arms slide right back down off of me and hit the floor. She does nothing to stop them. She's not awake. She might not even be alive. As I lean over again to pick her up, something hard and heavy hits my now shirtless back. "Shit, shit! Damn it! Fuck!" The scorching pain causes me to lurch up, knocking whatever it is to the ground. The only relief from the heat are the tears rolling down my cheeks. *We're never getting out of here.* I bend down again. *Fuck, that hurts!* I put my arms under her neck and scoop. Got her! I'm standing and I've got her! Which way now? Am I facing the right way, or did I spin around? Is that the hallway? Or is this the wrong way? *Think! You have to think!* My back is hotter than my chest, so the hallway must be in front. Or is that just because my back is burned? *You have to make a decision! Just go!*

Seventy-Six

JACOB

⚜

I clutch Olivia to my chest and stumble forward. "Olivia! Wake up!" I shout into her ear, hoping for a jolt, for a sign of life, for anything.

No answer. *Please let her be alive!* My shoulder crashes into the wall. Luckily Olivia's head is resting on my opposite shoulder. *Keep walking! Just keep moving!*

A doorway! I poke my head in. There has to be a window in this room, but where? It's too hard to see. Do I try to find it or keep going to the window I know is open? A fireball plummets from the ceiling, landing with a thump on the ground.

Decision made.

My grip on Olivia weakening, I press onward. Second doorway, same story. Can't see a thing. Just one more.

Fire jets up from the floor in front of us. A wave of heat rolls toward us, pushing me backward a step. There on the left. That's the door we need. If I can just squeeze by the flames, we'll be home free. Another wave of blistering heat crashes into me. Fuck! I smack the door open, coughing so hard I think I'm going to vomit. I push my way into the room, flinging the door shut behind us. My stomach clenches and heaves, but I manage not to throw up.

A new surge of energy propels me halfway across the room, then my right foot hits something and I stumble. Olivia starts sliding off my shoulder, but I catch her before her head smacks the ground. I start coughing again, and I'm not sure I have the strength to pick Olivia all the way back up. I drag her the rest of the way to the window. Hands under her armpits, I climb out of the window, then pull her out and into my arms. Taking steps as big as I can manage, I carry her away from the blazing house and set her as gently as I can on the ground.

"Come on, Olivia, wake up! You have to wake up!"

Olivia's cheeks are tinged red, as if sunburned, and blood is flowing from underneath her shirt. I lift the hem. *Shit, shit, shit.* That's where the bullet went in. I put one hand over the bullet wound and use the other to feel for her pulse.

No pulse.

No pulse.

No pulse.

The words reverberate in my skull, one per second, like a heartbeat. I close my eyes and remember the dream. Olivia flying. Us flying together. Trying desperately to hold on. Her fingers slipping through my fingers. Her body slamming into the ground.

She's dead. Just like in the dream.

If only I hadn't left her in the house. If only I had kissed her one last time. If only...

Fuck it. This is real life, not a dream. This isn't over. "Owen!" I shout. "Owen! Please come here!"

Owen opens the door of the truck warily. "I need you over here, Owen! Olivia needs your help!"

Those are the magic words. Owen leaps from the truck and dashes over to me. "What? What do I do? What's wrong with Olivia?"

"Put your hand here, buddy," I say, helping him cover the bullet wound with his small hand. "Now press down for me, okay? You're doing great."

Owen nods, way more composed than most adults would be. "Is that Olivia's blood?"

I nod, trying my best to remember my CPR from ninth-grade health class. Was it one rescue breath and then compressions? Suppressing the urge to cough, I tilt Olivia's head back and breathe air into her lungs. The effort throws me into a renewed coughing fit as I position myself above Olivia's chest, closing my eyes in a prayer that I've found the right spot. "And one and two and three and four and five..." This part of the training kicks in automatically.

Owen fixes his eyes on me. "Why are you counting? Are you playing a game?"

I shake my head, keeping up the count until I reach thirty, then I stop and give two rescue breaths, hoping I have the right sequence, fighting the nagging thought that I'm too late, that nothing can be done. I return to compressions, coughing too hard to count out loud.

"And one and two and three and four..." Owen's voice, strong and determined, keeps my count, even as blood seeps out underneath his palm.

As Owen reaches the end of the second set of thirty, a faint siren breaks through the sound of the river...and of the birds.

The birds...what did it all mean? All of the voices, the warnings that Olivia ignored, so certain that she was crazy.

The siren grows louder, filling my ears, blocking everything else out, and a vehicle roars up the driveway, kicking up a cloud of dust. Please let it be an ambulance.

Through the dust, I recognize the markings of a police car. Where's the ambulance?

The driver and his passenger throw open their doors, rushing over without bothering to slam the doors shut.

"We need an ambulance!" I shout, my voice cracking. "She's not breathing!"

"Get that man in cuffs!"

I recognize the voice. "Mom?"

The driver, a uniformed police officer, rushes over and slaps cuffs on Shipman. "What the hell?" The beast roars to life, struggling with the officer, who quickly gets him under control. "That girl burned down my house. I'm the victim here!"

"Get him in the back seat!" barks my mom.

"Jacob! Thank God!" To her credit, my mom doesn't give me shit for being here, for breaking every possible rule of common sense to come here on my own.

"Owen, honey, thank you so much for helping. You can take a break now. I'm going to help Jacob with Olivia."

Owen's lower lip trembles. "I don't need a break," he insists stubbornly.

My mom nods. "Okay, Owen, we can still use your help. Jacob, let me take over compressions. You help Owen cover that wound. But as soon as the paramedics get here, we're going to let them take over because that's their job. Okay, Owen?"

Owen nods vigorously. I move aside to let my mom take over and place my hand on top of Owen's, trying desperately to stop Olivia's blood from seeping between my fingers. I remember the first time that I saw Olivia at the restaurant, so confident, beautiful, and full of life. I see her in class, wearing my jacket, at the dance, in my arms. "Hang in there, Olivia."

A second siren builds in the distance. As I feel Owen's small hand under mine, for a moment I think it's my brother's hand.

This is Owen. Ben is gone.

I flash back to the image of Owen on the monitor and of Fuzzy, the stuffed animal my brother took with him everywhere, even to the park that horrible day. Over by the tree where I found Owen, I see Fuzzy is still there, propped against the trunk, looking abandoned. Why can't it be me on the ground, in Olivia's place? Why isn't it my blood on Owen's hands, my heart refusing to beat? My heart hurts so much I don't know how it can go on. I want so much to tell my mom about Ben, the words are fighting to get out, but I don't dare, because Olivia's very survival depends on the up-down motion of my mom's hands. Live. Breathe. Live. Breathe.

The ambulance is here. The paramedics stand beside me. "We've got it," they say.

I try to climb in the ambulance with Olivia, but they won't let me. They keep talking about my back, and they try to get me to lie down on my stomach on a stretcher.

Owen runs for Fuzzy, scoops him up into his arms, and hugs him close.

"Jacob?" I hear my mom's strangled cry as Owen runs back toward me.

My mom shakes her head, knowing she couldn't possibly be right. That the stuffed animal only looks like Fuzzy. Right then I feel the pain in my back. A pain so intense, it takes two paramedics to stop me from hitting the ground.

"Jacob? That's not...Of course it couldn't be..."

I'm looking right at her, but I can't answer.

Seventy-Seven

OLIVIA

Beep. Beep.

"Samantha?" My eyes fly open. "Samantha?" Warm fingers touch my hand. "Jacob? Is that you?"

"Well, good morning, Sleeping Beauty. It's about time you woke up. I'll text your mom. She's in the cafeteria."

"But, I thought…Samantha was just here. Are we…Is this…?"

"We're not dead, if that's what you're asking," Jacob says. "Although your heart did stop beating at one point, so technically…"

"I died."

Jacob nods.

"But you're okay. We're both okay. And Owen?" I ask, panic rising up inside me.

"Owen too."

"Thank God." I try to sit up.

"Careful, there. You've got to go slow. Here. I can adjust your bed." Jacob bends. He's wearing a hospital gown too. The back part hangs open at the top, and there's a huge white bandage near his shoulder.

"You're hurt. Did you get burned? Oh, God. This is all my fault. Are you going to be okay?"

"I'm fine. And it's not your fault. Nothing a few skin grafts can't fix."

"Skin grafts? No, no, no! I set that fire! Why did I set that fire? You're going to have a scar. Forever. You'll be…"

"Just like you? What's so bad about that?"

"I'm sorry, Jacob."

"Hey. It's better than being dead. Which is what I would have been. If you hadn't set that fire, Shipman would have shot me right then. So that fire? This scar. Thank you, Olivia." He squeezes my hand. "Here," he says, turning to a table next to me, "have a drink. Some nurse keeps changing out the water cups even though you haven't had a sip."

Jacob lifts a Styrofoam cup and aims the straw into my mouth. The cool water feels good, but my throat still feels raw.

"There had to have been a better way. I can't believe I set that fire. But Kevin did use the gun. He shot…me." I feel my arms, my legs. My stomach. "Here. He shot me here. But we were still in the house. How did I get out? Did you…Were you the one who…"

"I'll bring you some crayons, and you can make me an honorary firefighter's badge."

"But how? The door, it was covered in flames."

"The window. Same one you sent Owen out of."

"So that's how you got the burn?"

"Yep. Just some random crap from the room. But I prefer to think of it as a shooting star."

"You want to wreck the night sky like that?"

"Who says it's wrecked? No pain, no gain."

"Okay?"

"That might be the painkillers talking."

"Now that makes more sense." An ache pounds my side. I could use something too. So very tired. Just want to close my eyes. But first, there's something I have to know. "When you saw Owen on that monitor, you were talking about someone else..." I close my eyes and think as hard as I can. "Your brother, right?"

"That's right. Ben was my little brother's name."

"And Kevin Shipman, was he the one who took Ben?"

"Yeah. My brother and Owen were the only ones in Pennsylvania, but there were others that he took from all over the country." Jacob's voice cracks. "He sold them to the highest bidder on the dark web." Jacob looks up at the corner of the room and blinks repeatedly. "There were photos."

"But the fire. Wasn't everything destroyed in the fire?"

Jacob shakes his head. "Shipman stored them in a very safe place. Down in the bunker where he kept Owen. The firefighters stopped the fire before it reached down there. My mom and agents all over the country are tracking down what happened to the kids. They're hoping that this might be the lead that brings some of them home. A lot of families finally know the truth now—or at least part of it. Including mine."

I shift my weight, trying to get comfortable. "Is it better to know?"

"That's what they always say, right? That not knowing is the worst. That if only you knew the worst, you could at least move on." Jacob's eyes look heavy. "But when I didn't know, I could imagine that maybe my brother had been given to another family, some family desperate to have a child, and that he was living a good life and that maybe, just maybe, someday he'd come back to us. But he wasn't adopted, he's not alive, and some monster is the last person he ever saw. So no, knowing doesn't feel better right now. But at least we can stop hoping, I suppose."

"I'm sorry, Jacob. I'm really sorry."

He smiles weakly. "Thanks."

261

"What about Samantha? Who killed Samantha?"

"It was Shipman. He tried the bird drone before, when Samantha was babysitting. But she called Owen inside right then because it was bedtime. Owen said she thought it belonged to a neighborhood kid. In any case, she never said anything to the parents. But Shipman was afraid she had seen him, so he grabbed her and made it look like the Sweet Dreams killer."

I flash back to the first time I heard Samantha's voice, at her funeral. *Stop him.*

She hadn't been talking about the Sweet Dreams Strangler.

She was talking about Shipman.

It had been too late for Ben.

But because of her, and because of Jacob believing in me, it was not too late for Owen. And maybe, just maybe, not too late for someone else's child.

Seventy-Eight

JACOB

◈

S even years, four months, fifteen hours, and three minutes since the morning that my dad and I closed our eyes, we hold my brother's funeral. During the part where everyone walks around looking at pictures and sharing memories, I go up to my dad's wife.

"I just wanted you to know that I really do know your name," I say. "And I'm sorry that I've been such a jerk. I really can be a nice guy if I try."

"You are a nice guy, honey," she says, tears spilling out of the corners of her eyes. "And your dad just loves you to pieces," she says. "I hope you know that."

"Yeah, I guess I do," I say, and tears start spilling out of my eyes too, and I think it must be on account of my dad this time. My brother is a dull ache, a warm sunshine, a bittersweet memory.

I go up to my dad next and make the same apology. Then I add, "I thought maybe I could come live with you guys again. I promise I'll behave."

"As much as I'd love that, Jacob, your mother needs you now. She always did. She just didn't know how to show you that. And she knew I needed you more. I'll always be grateful to her for that. Okay? I mean, come for the summer, for a month maybe, and any weekend you want?"

I nod. I get it. He's right. Mom needs me more now. And Olivia is here.

But he keeps going. "It's not that I don't want you, I swear, Jacob. I love you. I'll fly you in anytime. Bring Olivia. Or I could buy you that Mustang, and you can drive—"

"Dad."

He takes a breath. I smile, making him smile.

"It's a deal," I say. "Me staying here, me visiting you…and me with a righteous red Mustang."

He laughs and ruffles my hair.

After the funeral, we go back to my mom's house. Well, my house. It's just my mom, Dad, and me. Sophia has excused herself, which seems pretty thoughtful on her part. In the living room are the boxes we brought up from the basement when we were looking for pictures of my brother for the funeral. And now we go through each and every box together as a used-to-be-family, and we talk about things like my brother's favorite food, chocolate pudding. We laugh about stuff, like the time Ben drove his construction truck through the flowerbeds and pulled out all of the flowers instead of the weeds, and we cry over the Elmo cake topper that was on his fifth birthday cake.

Though it takes us many hours, when we finish, we have three distinct piles: the things we're keeping to remember Ben by, the things we're taking to Goodwill, and the things we'll throw away. The first pile is small, as it should be, since there really is no way we could forget the little guy. The second and third piles my dad and I load into the car and then drive to their destinations. As for me, I keep the Elmo cake topper and the box of Legos, which I plan to give to Owen the next time I see him.

Seventy-Nine

JACOB

The wind blows me over to the cliff. I hover in the air, shaking my head at all the people lining up.

"Come on, everyone, back up. Stay away from the edge. You over there, you're too close. Back up! I said—"

Damn it! There goes another jumper. I'm sucked down with him. "Here, grab my hand!"

The old geezer looks up at me. He starts to put out a gnarled hand, then pulls it back. "Nah, forget it. I'm okay." He's smiling. "Really. Don't worry about it."

"Grab my hand! I mean it. You're about to die, man!"

He keeps grinning, until he hits the ground.

I wake up and turn on the light. Reach for my sketchpad. Record a man's passing. Feel grateful that the headaches have stopped. At least for now.

Right, who am I kidding? Dreams always seem real. But they're not. They're just not.

After all, Olivia jumped, but she didn't die.

Take that back. Her heart stopped. And then it started again.

My dream didn't lie. It just had a very fuzzy relationship with the truth.

Eighty

OLIVIA

o, Olivia, tell me how your voices are doing?" This is
Mindy talking. My shrink. I'm playing with this wire-bead
contraption she keeps on her desk.

"How they're doing? What, you mean, how they're feeling? We've
already established that they aren't real, haven't we?"

"Is that what you believe?"

I push one of the beads up its little hill and let it glide down. "Of
course that's what I believe. They were just my subconscious picking
up clues from discrepancies between what people said and what their
body language was telling me."

"How do you explain the birds and finding the necklace?"

I push another bead up and let it drop. "Owen must have mentioned
the bird. And finding Samantha's necklace, that must have been
because we both chose the same path to hike. I just wish I would
have realized it was hers at the time."

Mindy looks down at her nails as if she's rethinking the light pink polish she's chosen. "Does everyone feel this way?"

"Obviously not. My mom thinks I'm crazy. That's why I'm here, isn't it? I don't think Jacob knows what to believe. But his mom…"

"His mom?" she prods.

"Yeah, I think she believes in them. She gave me her card. Said to call her if I thought the voices were trying to give me clues to future crimes."

"You're laughing. Why?"

I wonder if it sounds like a normal laugh or an I'm-going-to-read-the-same-sentence-twenty-seven-times kind of laugh. "She's supposed to be the goddamn FBI! Since when does the FBI believe in ghosts?"

"She's also a mom. A mom who found out what happened to her son. Because of you."

"Why do I get the impression you're trying to make me believe in ghosts?"

"I'm just trying to get you to figure out for yourself what's going on."

"So you're not going to give me any drugs?" I push all of the beads back to the beginning.

"Do you want me to give you drugs?"

"What kind of question is that?"

"Have you been hearing voices since Kevin Shipman was captured?"

I take my time answering, first aligning the wire-bead thing with the edge of the desk. "No." It's kind of a lie, but only a half-lie. I haven't heard anything specific; it's been more like background noise. I hear people talking, but I can't make out any of the words. And I don't try either.

Lie or half-lie, I'm not sure why I don't tell my shrink the whole truth.

"Have you heard any voices telling you to harm yourself or others?"

"No." This time it's not a lie. Unless you count the voice that told me to set the fire. I'm not sure if that voice can be trusted.

"Then there's no reason to medicate you. If the voices come back, we can try medication, which may or may not help the voices go away. But the truth is, Olivia, you don't show any other signs of schizophrenia. The risk that you've developed the disease because your father had it is low."

And if I told you the whole truth, then what would you say?

Eighty-One

OLIVIA

'm not tired all the time anymore. Or cold. Also I haven't heard any voices in a while, not even that background noise, those voices I could hear without being able to make out the words. Nothing. I don't know whether they're gone for good, but I'm glad they're gone for now. At least I think I am.

Jacob and I haven't talked about my voices. Not since that day in the hospital. We also haven't talked about the fire I set. Or the fact that I had a Swiss army knife in my pocket that I might have used instead of the lighter. I haven't told him that a voice told me to set that fire. I haven't told anyone. They all believed me when I said the lighter was the only real choice I had, the only way I could think of to stop Kevin from shooting Jacob.

Maybe it was.

But maybe it wasn't.

Either way, I couldn't think because the voice telling me to start the fire was too loud.

Jacob and I have to talk about these things. But not today.

At seven the doorbell rings. It's Jacob here to pick me up for the movies. I'm not sure which movie—some comedy. We could both stand to laugh a little. As I open the door, Jacob grins down at me. "Hey, beautiful," he says. He kisses me, even though my mom is right there.

"Hey," I answer.

"Ready to go?"

"Yeah, I just need to put this wrapping paper back in the basement."

"Aw, you shouldn't have," Jacob teases, rubbing my shoulders.

"Nice try. It's for Julia's birthday. Unless you're planning on piercing your ears?"

"I'll pass. You brought all these rolls of paper up here to wrap that one little box?"

"It's too murky in the basement to see the colors properly."

"And that matters how?"

"It just does." I whack him on the head with a roll.

"Hey, watch it!" Jacob grabs a roll of his own and assumes a fighting stance.

"Maybe you guys could take that downstairs before you wrinkle it all up?" my mom suggests.

"My thoughts exactly." I give Jacob one last whack and then head for the stairs before he can retaliate. I make slow progress since my bullet wound is still sore, but Jacob is moving slow as well on account of the burn on his back. He does manage to whack me lightly on the head with his roll of wrapping paper, knocking a game off a shelf in the process.

It's the marble game. The marbles bounce and ping and scatter across the room. As Jacob watches the marbles spew out in all directions, I see him wince. "Shit. Of all the…"

"It's okay," I say. "It doesn't matter." I smile and bend down to help pick them up. We get most of them back in the box, and Jacob places it on the shelf.

"I see one more over by the drain. I'll get it. You can head out to the truck before my mom starts trying to practice her class lecture on you."

"Roger that," says Jacob, heading for the stairs. "Actually, I brought the Mustang." His eyes dance, bright and happy.

"Awesome." I'm glad Jacob forgave his dad. I wish I could forgive mine. I'm just not there yet.

I reach the drain. It's a green marble, and it's resting on one of the drain holes, like it belongs. Just as my fingers close around it, my ears get all buzzy. *No.*

I hear a voice. Coming from the marble.

A girl's voice.

Young.

I don't recognize it.

Help us, it says.

Help us.

Acknowledgements

This book is dedicated to Beverly and Ron. True love is eternal.

Thank you to Mike for following me up mountains in Switzerland, for trips to Ann Arbor in a powder blue sedan, and for ant traps. You can always make me laugh.

To Emily for heart-shaped pancakes, homemade wrapping paper, and cozy blankets. The things you create fill me with joy.

To Tim, who shares my love of words. You're my fashion idol, and I can't get your songs out of my head.

To Mary Lou and Jim for backyard badminton, building desks, and for never ever being mean.

To Brad and Angie for being our first (and best) babysitters, taking pictures of a certain prince, and letting our kids (and everyone else's) swim in your pool.

To Julie and John for always saving New Year's Eve for us.

To Melissa for always being there, and Art for the happiness he brings her.

To Peggy for helping me navigate the world of motherhood.

To Bob and Mary for your leadership and friendship.

Thanks to my aunts and uncles and cousins for a lifetime of memories, crazy times at the lake, and helping to promote my first book. I'm sure none of you will forget Grandpa's cannonball at our wedding.

Thank you, Kristin, for always being with me on this crazy journey. Your stories are beautiful and powerful.

To Heather for helping us all feel strong. Your novel in verse is breathtaking.

To Dawne, the organizer. Please write that novel about the singer!

To Julie, whose short story about diving gripped me from the very first word.

To Margaret, who with her novel will help give all women a voice.

To Lisa, who let me help name an amazing book that that will one day fill a special spot on my bookshelf.

To Shutta, who taught me that it's okay to send a book out into the world because there's another one inside waiting to be written.

To Ruth and Charlie, who are just fun to be around and supportive of everyone.

To Kevan, Deborah, Vicki, and Sherrie, the cheerleaders who helped make this book better.

To Monika, for the beautiful cover.

To the Apocalypsies, you all rock!

To writers who have books written only in their hearts—come on already, you can do it!

To readers, thank you for making writers' dreams come true.

About the Author

Tracy Bilen is the author of *What She Left Behind* and *Whisper*. She is a high school French teacher in Michigan where she lives with her husband and children. Tracy studied at the Sorbonne in Paris and taught Spanish at a high school ski academy. She loves biking, traveling, and red velvet cake.

You can connect with me on:

🜨 http://www.tracybilen.com

Subscribe to my newsletter:

✉ https://tracybilen.com/contact

CPSIA information can be obtained
at www.ICGtesting.com
Printed in the USA
LVHW032158240621
691066LV00006B/794

9 781735 352213